ONCE UPON A CHRISTMAS

A REGENCY MATCHMAKER SERIES
CHRISTMAS NOVELLA

MELYNDA BETH ANDREWS

PEDESTAL
BOOKS

PEDESTALBOOKS.COM

Once Upon a Christmas

a holiday story in

The Regency Matchmaker Series

ONCE UPON A CHRISTMAS

a historical romance

by

Melynda Beth Andrews

Once Upon a Christmas

a holiday novella in
the Regency Matchmaker Series

A PEDESTAL LANTERN BOOK

PUBLISHED BY PEDESTAL BOOKS

ISBN 978-1-947797-02-4 (paperback)
ISBN 978-1-947797-01-7 (ebook)

❧

.

The author asks that you neither participate in nor encourage piracy of this work. Other than for short excerpts for the purpose of critical review, this work may not be scanned, resold, lent, shared, or otherwise distributed without the express written permission of the author.

This is a work of fiction. All names, events, places, and persons are either used fictitiously, or they are products of the author's imagination and any resemblance to their real-life counterparts is entirely coincidental.

.

❧

For Lammer,
who handed down
her love of words
and elephants
and Christmases,
and
for the family
who loved her.

A Note from the Author

Dear Reader,

My characters keep having little adventures even after I write "THE END." These little stories are my gift to you. To get them, you just need to tell me where to send them. Go to

www.MelyndaAndrews.com

and sign up for my newsletter, *The Further Adventures*. I'll never share your email address, and I make it easy to unsubscribe at any time.

    I'm delighted you've chosen my work. I consider it an honor to entertain you, and I wish you many years of happy reading.

Yours,
Melynda

P.S. *The Further Adventures* are only available

to my subscribers. It's my way of saying, "Thank you!" Enjoy!

AN UNEXPECTED VISITOR

Stendmore Park, Buxley-on-Isis, England
December 18th, 1807

DAVID STENDMORE, THE Viscount Winter, skidded to a stop in the narrow doorway of the nursery at Stendmore Park. He glared in the direction of the wide, blue cushioned window seat, where his two daughters sat blinking innocently up at him, their rag dolls poised demurely on their laps.

David wasn't fooled.

"What was that thumping I heard *all the way down in the kitchen?"*

"Nothing, Papa," the girls chimed in unison.

"Humph!" David looked about the large, light-

filled room for evidence of mischief. Finding none, he glared down at Rose and Rain and tried to remind himself that his daughters' intent was never malicious. No, they were simply drawn to exploration, as he had been at their age.

Irresistibly drawn.

Incessantly drawn.

Disastrously drawn—and *where was Miss Bull?* It wasn't like her to leave the Hellions alone.

If the Viscount's daughters had inherited his taste for adventure, then it was fortunate they'd also inherited his old governess. Miss Bull was the Admiral Nelson of the nursery set. David had put her through her sea trials himself. Poor Miss Bull!

Raking his fingers through his tangled curls, he regarded his daughters with suspicion. They were being attentive and obedient—which meant they were up to mischief. Not that *that* was unusual. Rose and Rain were *always* knee-deep in mischief. Just like he'd been. As a lad, David had always been at the center of every spot of trouble. Hell, he'd been the cause of it, more often than not. And no one had any reason to think he'd changed.

Not yet.

"Where is our Miss Bull?" he asked evenly.

A look slid between his daughters. "We don't

know, Papa," Rose said, looking and sounding much more adult than her nine years should have allowed.

"She was reading a letter—" little Rain began.

"From this morning's post," Rose clarified.

"—an' she gave a cry like this." Rain screeched dramatically, bit her wrist, rolled her eyes into the back of their sockets, and slumped.

"Then she ran out," Rose said.

"Yes, Papa, she ran out. Just like that." Rain, just six, tried to snap her fingers, without success.

"Like *that*." Rose snapped her own fingers, winning a glare from her little sister. "She probably went to the necessary, Papa. All this excitement, you know," Rose said in sage tones, leaning close. "And speaking of excitement, should you not be below stairs? Preparing to receive our guests?"

"No," David said, waggling a finger. "I should be below stairs preparing to receive *my* guests. Mine— not *ours*. You two are not to leave this nursery during the house party unless flanked by a regiment of dragoons armed with sharp—"

"Papa!" the sisters chimed in perfect, indignant unison, though a sudden display of dimples spoiled their intended effect.

"All right!" He held up his palms in mock acquiescence. "I will garrison the regiment, but for the duration of the war that is my house party, you are still not to cross this threshold without an adult. There will be no more loud thumping and bumping up here, understand? You two will sit there and wait quietly for Miss Bull's return."

Rose and Rain nodded their solemn acceptance of his edict with too much alacrity. With their wide-eyed, innocent expressions, their shining brown hair, and their delicate little hands, they looked like charming angels, but the Viscount knew better. Charming hellions was what they were—though David loved them just the same, God help him. Love them? He shook his head in resignation. He didn't just love them. He adored them.

And he'd been a damned fool to stay away from them so long. A damned fool. They were his life— which was why this deuced, devilish house party was so important, and *where was Miss-blasted-Bull?*

There was so much to do before his guests arrived tomorrow. He hadn't a moment to spare. He was especially needed in the kitchen, where his undisciplined, untrained staff was sailing along without benefit of rudder, ballast, or keel. If he didn't get down there, he'd have naught to serve his guests but bread and cheese and ale!

David looked about the well-ordered nursery.

He didn't see much that could go wrong if he left to attend to the thousand-and-one things that needed his input. Miss Bull, who ran a tight ship, wouldn't be gone long, and the nursery, as always, was battened down for rough weather. The hearth stood cold and empty, with the tinderbox safely locked away in the cabinet—along with the poker, the ink bottles, and anything sharper than a spoon. The Hellions ought to be fine left alone for a few minutes.

And he *had* to get downstairs.

Though he could hardly hide Stendmore Park's strained circumstances from his guests, none but David realized the real danger. If a peer of the realm could not support his title and estate in such a manner that it brought honor to the Crown, the Crown could reabsorb them. It didn't happen often, but it was not unknown—and David was at low tide and on somewhat less than friendly terms with Prinny, who had a little too much influence. David had to secure a hasty loan or two, which was why he'd called the house party.

He had to convince the surrounding gentry, from whom any loans would come, that he'd changed. His children's futures depended upon it.

"You are still glaring, Papa." Rain's expression

was full of genuine concern. She was a surprisingly compassionate child, considering her mischievous nature. "What's wrong?"

"My cravat is too tight, that is all." There was no need to worry them. Offering a smile of truce, he tousled Rose's curls, pinched Rain's cheeks, and then he made to leave—but as he turned his back, he thought he saw a look pass between them.

A conspiratorial look, a mischievous look, a look that foretold doom.

David crossed his arms and scowled some more, and their eyes widened, but as he opened his mouth to interrogate them, a flash of blue outside the window caught his eye. Against the dull blacks and browns of winter, Miss Bull's blue gown stood out plainly. She was crossing the lawn far below. Craning his neck, he moved to the window to watch. What was she doing down there?

It was no matter. She was heading toward the back of the house, now. No sense in tempting fate. He'd wait right here in the nursery for her to—

He stilled as he got a better look at the woman. It wasn't Miss Bull. This was a much slimmer woman, and she was dressed in a stylish frock, not in one of Miss Bull's somber gowns. And, come to think of it, he'd never seen Miss Bull in blue. She always wore some shade of gray or brown.

As the mystery woman moved closer, he discerned that she carried a small portmanteau, and shock coursed through him. Could she be one of his guests? Perhaps her carriage had arrived early, and with no one at the front door to receive her, she'd ended up in the stable yard. She could also be a villager he supposed. There was no way to be certain, but one thing *was* certain: the woman's current heading was going to take her sailing right in through the back door, which led to the chaos that was his kitchen!

"Bloody hell!" he cried, forgetting where he was.

"I thought hell was supposed to be fiery," Rose said, "not bloody."

Rain wrinkled her nose in disgust, but then a keen look came into her eyes. "Where'd the blood come from, Papa?"

His gaze didn't leave the window as he shook his head violently and held up one hand. "No, no. I did not mean—"

"It comes from fallen angels, I wager," Rose interrupted him. "It's a long way from Heaven to— down there," she finished in a whisper-that-was-not-a-whisper. "They must bang themselves up when they fall."

Rain's eyes widened. "Do they get scraped knees?"

Rose nodded enthusiastically. "And bloody noses! And bulging eyeballs! And—"

"Enough!" David's head was pounding. "You will wait here for Miss Bull, and you will not cross that threshold!"

Rose's eyes narrowed. "What if there is a raging fire, Papa?"

"Or if we cut ourselves?" Rain added.

The woman below still hadn't tacked away from her course.

"Fire and blood are the only exceptions. You see those, and you are free young ladies."

Rose's eyes flicked toward her sister and lit up. "Blood?"

"Yes," David said. *"Yours*. At least enough to fill a thimble."

"Oh," came Rose's dejected reply.

David again raked his fingers through his hair, tangling them in his unbrushed curls, and sighed. He had a valet who preferred a liquid breakfast, a butler and housekeeper who'd run away to Gretna

Green, and now his governess had gone a-roving. Perfect. What was next?

What was next was that the young woman set down her portmanteau and reached for the kitchen door.

David groaned. "Pray, let her not be one of the guests!"

"Oh!" the gregarious Rose cried, while her shy little sister squealed and hid under the bed. "Truly, Papa?" Rose breathed. "One of our guests? Already? I did not fancy any had yet arrived!" She pressed her nose against the glass,

David pivoted and ran. "Away from that window!" he called over his shoulder. "And *do not cross this threshold!*" He charged through the door and down the hallway.

2

NO MATTER WHAT THEY SAY

HEN DAVID WALKED into the kitchen affecting a calm he did not feel, the young woman was already there. To his surprise, she was seated at the wide, oaken table, attacking a mug of milk and an enormous bowl of porridge, and upon closer inspection, David saw that her dress, though not unfashionably cut, had seen better days. Torn and dirty, it was muddy and damp at the hem. Her portmanteau wasn't in any better shape.

So, she was a beggar, not a guest. David wilted in relief.

Cook hastened over to him. "I hope you don't mind, my lord," she said, so that only he could hear.

"I know we don't have much to spare, but look at her. The poor mite is half starved."

Though the young woman didn't look especially emaciated to David, she did look hungry. She hadn't even looked up as he'd entered. "I have no objection, of course," he said. "Pray keep her bowl and mug filled for as long as she can empty them."

"That I will, and gladly." Cook lowered her voice even more. "She looks like a *lady*, if you ask me, sir," she said. 'That ain't no calico her gown's made of, and I—" She gave a sudden shriek. "My *sauce!*" She rushed to the stove, but she was too late. A pot boiled over with white stuff. An unpleasant odor permeated the room as the sauce hit the iron plates of the stove. Cook wrapped a piece of leather around the pot's handle and pulled it from the heat, then grabbed a spoon and stirred furiously, but it was apparently no use. "It's burnt!" she cried. "I'll *never* get this right!"

David was inclined to agree. Though he didn't know how to cook fine food, he knew it when he tasted it, and precious little of Cook's food qualified. Not surprising, as she'd been but a scullery maid until David promoted her barely a month ago. No matter. It could not be helped. There was no time to hire another cook, and there was no money for it anyway.

Cook shoved the pot aside in disgust. "Ruined," she said.

"Flour and butter we have plenty of," David said. "Try again."

"Yes, my lord," she sighed. "But before I do, will you take a look at these?" She wiped her hands on her apron and retrieved a sheaf of papers from a side table. "The menus for the party," she said, thrusting the papers into his hands.

"Show them to Miss Channing," David said with a dismissive wave.

"I did, sir. She said I was to show them to you, begging your pardon."

David sighed and took the papers to the window to catch the morning light. Miss Channing, his new housekeeper, had been but a downstairs maid a month ago, an astonishing leap in responsibility. But, again, it could not be helped. Out of necessity, half of the now-senior members of his staff had been promoted in the same manner.

Six months ago, he'd come home from a long sea voyage to find Stendmore Park in chaos. A fever had swept over the countryside the year before, taking many good people.

Including his brother.

David sighed heavily and flipped to the back of the page he was examining. After Robert was buried, half of his staff had simply drifted away, not that he blamed them. Wages had gone unpaid for almost a year and the house unprovisioned for weeks. David's homecoming meal had been the best the diminished and beleaguered staff of Stendmore Park could offer: dry bread and cheese, washed down with the stable master's good ale. And things weren't much better now, six months later.

Everything still balanced on the knife-edge of ruin. Everything.

A movement at the kitchen table pulled David's tired eyes from the menus. A kitchen maid was serving the beggar another measure of porridge. Something about her caught his attention, and David watched as the maid finished ladling the plump oats into her bowl. The young woman sat with her back straight, her hands folded politely on top of the napkin on her lap, as the maid served her. Then she inclined her head and murmured her thanks, and David knew instantly from her manner that the young woman was accustomed to being waited upon.

Impoverished gentry, he supposed, though he

did not know of a lady of her years living near Buxley. She was perhaps two or three years younger than David himself—call her five-and-twenty? She had to have come from some distance. She was in narrow straits indeed if she were traveling unaccompanied a long distance on foot. Who was she? And how had she landed in such a remote place?

Though the conundrum was intriguing and his sympathy aroused, David simply had no time to waste. Pondering her circumstances was a luxury he couldn't afford.

And yet …

As he watched her slender fingers curl around one of the kitchen's coarse stoneware mugs and lift it to her soft, bow-shaped mouth, he found himself setting the menus down upon the wide windowsill and approaching her. Her delicate, white hands looked more accustomed to playing the pianoforte than working or begging. There wasn't a callus on them.

He had horses to spare and groomsmen enough. Perhaps if her destination was not too far away, he could be of service. She stood as he approached, and David bowed. "I am David Stendmore, the Viscount Winter. Welcome to Stendmore Park."

She curtsied and inclined her head gracefully. 'Thank you, my lord."

He expected her to introduce herself, but the seconds ticked by, and she said nothing. "Where are you headed?" he asked.

"I come from the North," she averred. "I have no definite plans."

No definite plans. "Who are you?" he asked, deliberately blunt.

"I am no one." Her words carried no trace of impertinence. It was a fact, clearly stated.

"You used to be someone," he said, "and recently, I reckon. Have you no family?"

Her deep brown eyes became hard. "My name is … Emily Jones, my lord, and my past … is my own. Do you wish me to leave now?"

He felt an urge to smile at her defiance, but he beat it down. "Your bowl is still full of porridge, Miss Emily Jones. I would not want you to waste it. Pray stay as long as you wish."

She threw him a mischievous smile. "That you cannot mean." There was no shame in her expression, and her eyes were intelligent.

"I daresay Stendmore Park can spare a few bowls of porridge, Miss Jones. You may stay in the barn a day or two if you wish."

She nodded her thanks and smiled. It was a pretty smile, a ladylike smile, and David winced at the thought of a gently brought up young woman sleeping in a barn — *his* barn! — but he couldn't very well invite a gently brought up young woman to stay under his roof unchaperoned, now, could he? Not that she likely had much of a reputation to ruin, but he did not want to risk having something go horribly wrong that necessitated *marrying* the chit. His girls needed a mother, to be sure, but not just any woman would do.

"My lord?" the cook prompted. "I still need to walk into Buxley Village to place orders."

"Of course," David said, retrieving the menus. "But I am afraid the menus will need some modification before you strike out for the village."

"I *knew* it," Cook said, dejected. "The menus ain't good enough. I'll never make it as cook."

David shook his head. "You will, because you must. I'll have no more talk of failure. See here ... is this wine you have listed here the best we have?"

"Why, yes, my lord. It is the very best we have, of course! And I'm told it's good stuff, for the late Viscount kept a first-rate cellar, beggin' your pardon, sir."

"Mmm, yes." David did not doubt it. "Cook, during this house party, please do not serve our guests the best of the wine. Instead, serve the worst quality we have, unless it has turned to vinegar."

"The *worst* quality, my lord?"

"Our guests must not fancy me extravagant."

"Yes, sir. What about the rest of the menu, sir?"

David tapped the paper. "I am afraid the food goes the other direction. Too plain. Plenty of mutton and game, but no beef. Ample cream—but where are the spices and the sweets? We must have a Christmas pudding at the very least. And are there not other dishes our guests will expect to be served? Special Christmas dishes?"

"Oh, indeed there are, sir. Wassail and frumenty and Christmas pies."

"Sugar plums!" a maid offered.

"Gingered nuts and shortbread," said another, and the rest of the kitchen staff chimed in.

"Trifle!"

"Twelfth Night Cake!"

"Syllabub!"

"Ooh," breathed Cook. "Heavens, yes! Syllabub. I love syllabub." She clapped her hands together in delight before dropping them to her sides and knitting her brows. "Though I don't know how to make it." She heaved a sigh. "And that ain't the only trouble." Moving to turn her back to the others, Cook bent closer to David. "None of it can be made without us laying in more sugar and spices, and there ain't enough money for more spices and sugar, my lord. Nor beef."

As soon as she'd bent toward him, all movement in the kitchen had stopped, and though she'd taken care to whisper, Cook's voice had carried to every straining ear. They were awaiting his response.

"Sell some more silver."

Cook flicked a glance at Miss Jones and David flinched. He'd forgotten she was there. He felt an inexplicable jolt of shame as he glanced over at her.

She was staring at him with an expression of sympathy.

A burst of movement rescued him from framing some sort of response as Miss Bull burst into the room. She wasn't in truth old—not even fifty yet—but David had been right and tight she was older than God when he was a lad.

"Oh, Master David!" she cried, waving a letter, her eyes full of panic and tears.

David took her hand. "Why, Miss Bull! What is the matter?"

"It is my mother." She waved the letter some more. "She is frightfully ill." Her eyes implored him.

"You must go to her at once, of course." Turning to a footman, he ordered, "Have the coach brought 'round. Make haste!"

Miss Bull's expression registered relief. "You always were a good boy," she crooned. "No matter what they said."

David's eyes flicked toward the beggar.

They? The question hung in her eyes like a Christmas star, bright and clear.

Miss Bull patted his hand. "I am sorry to leave you at a time like this, my boy, and I shall return as soon as may be."

"Do not trouble yourself, my dear Miss Bull. Take all the time you and your mother need. I pray she will recover fully."

The governess hurried from the kitchen.

"Poor thing," Cook remarked after Miss Bull was gone. "There ain't no good time to be sick, but Christmastime is the worst."

As murmurs of general assent filled the kitchen, David's eyes again met the beggar's, and he allowed his face to break into an easy grin. It was a social ploy, a deflection, a tool he'd used so many times in the past that it came to him now without thinking about it, but his grin didn't work this time. Miss Jones averted her gaze, yet not before David could discern a deepening of the lines on her forehead.

A sudden tumult erupted somewhere in the front of the house, saving him from framing any sort of response as the hallways echoed with the sounds of arrival. It was a barking, whining, nail-on-marble-and-wood sound that could only mean one thing: Sir Basil and Lady Griselda!

Their arrival was confirmed a moment later by Mr. Crabbe, his new butler, who'd been but a footman a month ago. "No one is supposed to arrive until tomorrow, my lord!" he protested. "I have a copy of the invitation right here in my pocket. I wrote them out myself. It says clearly, 'Saturday, the eighteenth of December.' And that's tomorrow."

A strangled sound escaped David. "Today is *Friday* the eighteenth," he said, "not *Saturday!*"

"Oh, dear! I wrote the wrong date, didn't I?"

David nodded. "And at least some of the guests won't notice your mistake and will be arriving today!"

Poor Mr. Crabbe looked miserable. "I wish I could melt into the floor." At that moment, Cook fainted and folded into a surprisingly gentle heap. "Nice try," Crabbe muttered.

The scullery maids dashed for the hartshorn and collided, Sir Basil's seven mongrel dogs came charging into the kitchen — with their master not far behind, judging by the voice booming down the hall — and, outside, a flash of white heralded the fall of a bed sheet rope from the nursery window. The Hellions were attempting to escape!

In one smooth motion, David launched himself into action, snatching a plate of stale buns from a cupboard and rolling the lot down the hall. The dogs dashed after the things, snarling and shoving, effectively blocking Sir Basil's progress toward the kitchen. "Dash around front and divert Sir Basil and Lady Griselda's attention!" he ordered Mr. Crabbe, and the young man rushed off to comply.

David ran out the back door. "What are you doing?" he shouted up at the nursery window.

"We are coming outside to play," came a small voice.

"And what did I tell you about leaving the nursery?"

"You told us not to cross the threshold."

"Stay right there!" Raking his hand through his errant hair, David dashed back into the kitchen. "Where is Rachel?" he demanded of the staff, referring to a kitchen maid. She could watch the children. She was particularly large and disconcertingly burly.

The youngest kitchen maid answered, "She's helpin' young Tom cut the Yule log, sir."

"The Yule log!" David rolled his eyes. It was bad enough that he had to press under-gardeners into service as footmen. Now he had serving maids out cutting timber. "Remind me to pay her an extra week's wage—when I can afford it," he added under his breath.

"Papa?" Rain called faintly from the window.

"What!"

"Are you sure we cannot climb down just once? We shall climb right back up again."

"You are not to climb through that window! Or any other window," he added. "Or the chimney. Disassemble that rope and make up your beds immediately!" He turned to the staff with a feeling of mounting desperation. "Can any of you tie knots?"

"Aye," said one of the scullery maids. "I can." She wasn't a timid young waif. She looked strong and even a little mean.

"Then you'll do."

"For what, my lord?"

"You are promoted to nursemaid until Miss Bull returns. All you have to do is watch my daughters and see they do not find trouble."

A happy smile blossomed over the maid's face, but Cook, who had recovered, blustered, "No, no! Begging your pardon, my lord, but you can't take Betsy! I've only got two kitchen maids as it is. If you take her, there'll be no one to wash up. What about the china and the crystal and the pots and the silver?"

A loud thump emanated from the open nursery window. David asked Cook, "Is there no other help available?"

"None, my lord. Mr. Crabbe, Miss Channing, and I have all scoured the countryside three miles 'round. There are none who will take a position here with no wages forthcoming and—er ... and all."

David sighed. *And all,* indeed!

Stendmore Park barely had enough to feed its staff, and the fare was only barely edible, from time to time. Even the beggars had stopped coming to the back door. All except for the young lady thoughtfully chewing and watching him with unconcealed curiosity.

An even louder thump and a crashing sound rent

the air. "Nothing broke!" chimed two little-girl voices.

The butler scurried into the kitchen, all seven dogs in his wake. "Sorry, my lord, but Sir Basil insists upon seeing you straightaway!"

"I say!" a booming voice echoed down the hall. It was Sir Basil. "Friends such as we do not stand on ceremony!"

David had known good Sir Basil since he was a boy. He and his lady wife lived in the next village, and David had been hard-pressed to avoid receiving them thus far. It had been rude of him, but it had also been unavoidable. He'd known the first night he'd come home what he'd have to do to resurrect Stendmore Park.

"Where is the Viscount?" Sir Basil called. "Deuced fine of him to invite us to the house party. Deuced fine! Where is he? My lady and I want to thank him and congratulate him on his homecoming. First rate, first rate!" Sir Basil's voice was growing louder.

David raked his hand through his hair—and then his eyes lit upon the beggar yet again. She now had the good grace to have most of her face hidden behind an ancient, tattered copy of *La Belle Something-or-Other*.

"You there, Miss Jones!"

Her brown eyes popped over the top of the magazine. "Me?"

"Yes. You have no place to stay." It was a statement, not a question. "Have you employment?"

"None."

"Good. I need a temporary governess. You are hired." He turned to Mr. Crabbe. "See that she's shown to the nursery," he said as a third loud thump reverberated through the house. "Quickly," he added, and out of the kitchen he charged. "Sir Basil!" his voice rang down the hall. "How good to see you!"

EMILY SAT, BEMUSED. Imagine, the daughter of none other than Cornelius and Patricia Winthrop, being offered employment! As a governess!

The kitchen staff quickly turned back to their work, and Emily was struck by the panic in their movements. What was going on here? But she had no time to ponder the conundrum.

"Come on, then." The butler—Mr. Crabbe, was it?— motioned to Emily impatiently. "Let us find a maid."

Emily put down the ladies' magazine and sat very still for a moment. What was she to do now? Become an impromptu governess?

She looked out the small kitchen windows at the bleak winter landscape. It was cold outside, she had nothing to eat, she had no money left, and the dirty gown she was wearing was the cleanest of the three she had with her. If she'd been a real impoverished gentlewoman, being offered a temporary position as governess would be a godsend. But she wasn't. She was Miss Emily Winthrop, the eldest daughter of the Winthrops of Windlay Square, whose vast fortune and no sons to inherit guaranteed Emily's future many times over. Taking on employment as governess was the last thing anyone would expect of her. The very idea of was laughable.

On the other hand, perhaps the odious Duke of Besshire wouldn't want her once she'd been *employed*.

She rose and smiled. Everything was going to be fine. Not that she'd ever had any real doubt it wouldn't be—though this morning *had* stretched the boundaries of that faith. She'd been hungry and cold and tired when she'd approached Stendmore Park. But she'd told herself the night was always darkest just before the dawn, and she had never given up hope. It just wasn't in her nature.

Retrieving her small portmanteau from outside the kitchen door, she scurried after the short butler and through the winding halls of the enormous, rambling house, being careful to avert her face from open doorways.

Sir Basil and his wife Lady Griselda were a merry pair, a frequent addition to the ballrooms of London, where Emily had been seen often enough of late. And while they were old, their eyesight was keen, and their minds were keener.

It would not be at all The Thing to be recognized, which she surely would be, should she come face-to-face with any of London's *beau monde* — even as dirty and unkempt as Emily was. She would just have to stay out of sight, which shouldn't be too difficult, she reasoned, seeing as she was but a country governess. She would not be expected to dine with the family, not during a Christmas house party, at any rate.

She smiled. Everything would be fine. Everything was perfect. Like a circus acrobat, she'd leapt into the air, and a net had appeared!

There was just one tiny problem—well, one rather largish problem, truth to tell, but that problem was hidden out in the barn, and the stable master had already offered to help Emily keep it out of sight.

3

WILD AND WILLFUL

I T HADN'T BEEN hard to convince the stable master to help her, for the good man dearly loved animals, and the chance to care for a poor, mistreated baby elephant for a half-hour or so had proved too much for him to resist. Emily was a good judge of character, and she'd have bet her last guinea—if she hadn't already spent it—that he wouldn't balk too much about having to billet the elephant in the stable for a week or so, just until the real governess returned.

"Bantlings!" Gertie, a very young maid, called as they entered the nursery. "Miss Rose, Miss Rain, this is your new governess, Miss ..." She turned to Emily. "Pardon me, miss. What did you say your name was?"

Two sets of eyes peered from behind the nursery curtains, and the Viscount's daughters wrinkled their noses. "Our new governess?" the taller girl asked, her eyes round.

"New governess!" the younger one echoed. "Bully is dismissed?"

Bully?! Emily shook her head. "It isn't like that," she began, but her sentence was drowned out by the cheering, whooping, squealing dance of two smiling, shouting little girls.

"They're heartbroken," Gertie remarked dryly. "These, in case you have not guessed, are your charges, Miss Rose Stendmore" —she inclined her head toward the taller girl— "and Miss Rain Stendmore."

"Thank goodness!" Rose cried.

"It worked!"

"What worked?" Emily asked.

"The spiders," Rain said, earning an elbow in her side and a glare from her big sister. "Oh," Rain corrected herself. "Nothing."

Gertie gave Emily a sidelong look. "Good luck," she muttered.

"I am afraid that spiders had nothing to do with Miss Bull's absence," Emily said, trying not to laugh. "I am only here temporarily."

The girls groaned. "How long is 'temporarily?'" asked Rain.

"Only until 'Miss Bully' returns."

Both girls giggled and covered their mouths, and then the eldest asked, "When will that be?"

"It is uncertain. Her mother is ill, and she has traveled to be with her. I could be here a few days or a few weeks, I suppose."

The girls looked at each other and grinned. "Weeks!" both shouted. Their eyes shone, and Emily wondered why. Miss Bull hadn't seemed the sort of dragon to inspire such disloyalty. In fact, downstairs in the kitchen, she'd seemed to possess an almost motherly tenderness for the girls' father. So why did his daughters despise her so much?

Emily looked about the room. It was a large, well-appointed space with tall, bright windows, thick carpets, and good, solid furnishings. Nothing amiss there. But, as she surveyed her surroundings, it suddenly occurred to her that it wasn't the sort of room one would expect housed children.

Where were the drawings? The birds' nests? The sea shells? Where were the toys? The storybooks? The dried-up old daisy chains?

Where was the mess?

"My," Emily said, "how … tidy everything is!"

Rose and Rain slid each other a look. "Do you like things to be tidy?" Rose asked, her face wary.

"Well ... yes, but this ..." Emily began. Clasping her hands behind her back, she walked slowly along a long, low row of bookcases, her back straight, trying to look like an officer surveying his troops. Down at the last bookcase, she ran one finger across its top and examined the dust she found there. "It is not as clean as I would wish ..."

Behind her, she heard the girls groan again.

"And," she said, "it is entirely too tidy."

"What?" exclaimed the maid.

"Yes." Emily turned. "I detest tidy nurseries. The neater they are, the less learning takes place." She turned to the girls. "It is clear your minds have been idle. I want you to get busy. Create a mess. At once!"

"In truth?"

"Do you mean it?"

"I mean what I say. Go forth and play. I want to see several toys scattered about, several storybooks out on the table, and several pictures drawn by the time I return."

Rain clapped her hands excitedly. "I *like* her!"

Rose wasn't listening. She'd made a dash for the bookshelf.

"Uh ... where are you going?" the maid asked nervously.

"With you," Emily said, watching the girls with a satisfied smile on her face. "You are going to show me to my bedchamber."

The maid threw a baleful look in the girls' direction. "Do you fancy leaving them alone is wise?"

Emily smiled. "Not to worry, Gertie. Look at them."

The girls were already hard at work, both silent, with looks of intense concentration on their faces. It was obvious Miss Bull was a stern and unforgiving taskmaster. One look at the austere nursery had told Emily the sort of life these little girls led. Much too restrictive. "I expect they shall be too busy playing to make mischief. My chamber, if you please."

The maid lifted one eyebrow and shrugged, a gesture that clearly said, *'So be it. It is on your head, not mine!'* "Right through this connecting door, miss." She led the way. "Afraid it's quite small."

"No matter," Emily said, following Gertie into the sparsely furnished chamber. "It is a vast improvement over what I have been used to."

It was true. For most of a month, Emily had been sleeping at inns, farmhouses, crofters' cottages, and, after her money had run out a few days ago, barns or haystacks. To her, the well-appointed room looked heavenly. It held a sturdy bed with soft green hangings, a dressing table, a small sofa sandwiched between the window and the hearth, and a wardrobe—not that she had much to put into it. Emily placed her portmanteau on the counterpane and began to open it.

"Here, let me take that," Gertie said and began to unpack for her, clucking at the condition of Emily's two spare gowns and other things as she took them out of the portmanteau. Emily winced in embarrassment. Her clothes hadn't been properly laundered in a fortnight.

Before Gertie finished the job, a second maid came into the room with an enormous armload of clothing.

"The master had these sent up for you, miss. I took it upon myself to order you hot water brought up. You'll have it in a bit."

She left, and Gertie began to hang the clothing in the wardrobe. "I daresay," she remarked, looking Emily up and down, "these gowns should fit just about right. All but certain places, but those can be taken in. Or plumped up a bit sneaky-like, if you take my meaning."

It was an indelicate observation, to say the least, and Emily turned away to hide a smile. Lord Winter's staff was raw, indeed. This maid was young and untrained, but she was pleasant enough, and Emily decided she liked her.

"The gowns are lovely," Emily remarked. "But whose are they?"

A pained look appeared on the little maid's face. "I hope you won't take no offense, ma'am. They belonged to his lordship's wife. His dead wife," she clarified. "She died of childbed fever right after Miss Rain was born."

"Oh! Those poor children!" Emily shook her head. "Ah … will Lord Winter not find the sight of the clothes disturbing?" she asked the maid.

"No … they say his lordship hardly ever saw his wife."

"Never?"

"Well, twice, at least." Gertie grinned. "Just long enough to get the girls, and then off he went, apparently."

"He served in the army, did he not?"

Gertie shook her head. "The navy. But not before he cut quite a swath through London, I hear tell." She looked around and lowered her voice, warming to the subject. "They say he was a very naughty lad there in London." She waggled her eyebrows.

"Mmm," Emily intoned noncommittally. News of the infamous David *Spendmore* had been all the talk in London a few months earlier, after his elder brother had passed and the new Viscount had returned to England. But a rakehell viscount wasn't a proper subject for unmarried ladies, apparently, so Emily didn't know much detail. She'd heard whispered snippets of wild rumours—the most titillating and tantalizing of which concerned a certain duchess and a peacock feather!—but all she knew for certain was that he was a widower who'd inherited his title upon his brother's death and returned from somewhere after a long absence and that he'd earned himself a reputation as a rakehell long before that.

"Naughty how?" Emily asked before reminding herself that she shouldn't be interested in such gossip.

"Oh, all sorts of ways!" She laughed. "Must have vexed his parents, too. Right cold fish they were."

"Mmm."

"Misers. Went way beyond frugal. Didn't believe in boisterous carryings-on. That always led to spending money. No parties, no holiday feasts, no Boxing Day. And when their boys came along, they even stamped out music and dancing! The poor mites—they weren't allowed no high jinks at all. Why, I hear they didn't even burn a Yule log nor hang mistletoe at Christmas! And I believe it, for the kitchen don't even have a pudding pot!"

"Oh dear!" Emily said, forgetting she wasn't interested.

"Miss Bull was their governess, too, though she's a warmer sort than their parents must have been. She don't put up with anything nonsensical, though."

Emily nodded. She knew how that was. Her own governess was that way as well. And her parents. "When parents hold the reins too tight, the children pull at the bit," she said.

"Aye." Gertie nodded. "That's so."

"I suppose Lord Winter always was a wild one, then?"

"Oh, no, I don't fancy so, miss. It's said both lads tried hard to please their parents—though young Master David was always up to some mischief, Miss Bull says. He never did manage to curry favor as did Master Robert."

A pair of footmen came in bearing a small metal

wash-tub and buckets of steaming water, which Gertie directed them to place on the hearth as she lit the fire. Closing the door after they left, she helped Emily undress and bathe.

"Not that being their favorite did Master Robert any good in the long run," she said out of the blue, as though their conversation had not been interrupted.

"What happened with him?" Emily asked, no longer even attempting to feign disinterest. She found she liked being a governess. A governess could ask questions and expect to get answers, it seemed.

"Oh, he rebelled," Gertie said. "Both of the lads did, though Robert was first. It was fast horses and even faster emptying of bottles for him. But Master David still tried to be a good boy—for a while."

"And then what?"

"Well, after a turn, he learned what was intended for him. He was the spare, not the heir, you see, and they expected to bundle him off to Northumberland or some such outlandish place where a cousin o' theirs had a living to bestow. I guess Master David was to take it and be a country parson. But he took the legacy left him by his old gaffer and hied off to London instead. Threw over his traces spectacular-like."

"Oh my!"

Gertie laughed and went on. "Squandered the lot, they say, on all manner of vices. Had himself a fine time! And when the money was gone, he up and joined the Navy to displease his father and married beneath him to displease his mother. Stopped home only long enough to deposit his wife here before he went to sea."

"What was she like?"

"The missus?" The maid smiled. "Quiet. Shy. A timid little thing, but pleasant enough. No family whatsoever. He found her somewhere in London." She lowered her voice to a whisper. *"In a bawdy house!"*

Emily's eyes widened, and Gertie laughed again, obviously relishing her subject. "It's said it was her first week ... ah ... *on the job*, so to speak, and he married her as much to rescue her as to displease his parents. She were a common little thing. Plain as a post, too. But sweet as they come."

Emily looked down at her hands and changed the subject. "Ah ... wasn't she unhappy to be left alone here?"

"There are some who say she didn't mind,"

Gertie whispered. "Some say she and Master Robert fell in love." She clamped her lips together for emphasis. "There, now! You're all clean. How about choosing a dress? I dare say this one will do," Gertie said without waiting for a response from Emily. "You'll look fine in it." She held up a gown with a white, lace-trimmed bodice and bright blue skirts. "There's even a shawl to match, I think," she said, sorting through the other clothes. "Yes. Here it is."

Emily laid the shawl on the bed and began to dress. It felt strange wearing another woman's clothes, but they were fresh and clean, and, again, it was an enormous improvement over what she'd had.

Once more, things were working out just right.

"How long has Lord Winter been home again?" she asked.

"Oh ... six months, give or take. But you're making me get ahead of myself. There's more to the story. The influenza struck the countryside two summers ago. I was but thirteen, which worried my own mama something fierce, thirteen being an unlucky number and all. Yet I was spared where a couple dozen others weren't, so I can't see as how it's all that unlucky, can you?"

Emily shook her head.

"Stendmore Park lost close on a dozen,

including the Viscount's brother." She clucked her tongue. "It was a sad state of affairs, and no mistake. I'm glad I wasn't old enough to be working up here, then. Wages unpaid and cellars bare. And none hereabouts knew what to think when the new Lord Winter come. We didn't know if we was in the frying pan or the fire, if you take my meaning. He was so Friday-faced." She shuddered. "They say he changed after Trafalgar. War is hard, even for Navy men like him. He's grim-like and cold most of the time. Like his parents, I reckon."

She worked on Emily's hair for a few moments, before saying, "They say the apple don't fall far from the tree, and I guess that's so. Still and all, he seems to care what goes on hereabouts. He's raised a good many of us up in our positions, when he might have called in more-experienced help, and everybody knows he's putting things to rights as much as he can. Still not paying wages yet, but we're all fed. Betwixt us, I fancy he'd have left the place to rot if it weren't for Wild and Willful."

"Who?"

"His little 'uns. Rose and Rain. Uncouth little things, ain't they? Not that it's their fault, mind you."

"Are they ... are they unkind?"

"No, just high-spirited. Like him when he was a boy, I hear tell. Now, then, don't you look lovely?" She turned Emily around to peer in the looking glass.

Emily hardly recognized herself. Her hair was pulled up in a simple bun with no ribbon or ornament. Her clothes were plain and unadorned with jewelry. She *looked* like a governess! Her mother and father would be mortified.

Good!

"Well, if you won't be needing anything more from me, miss, I'd best be getting downstairs. And you'd best be getting back to the nursery."

"All is quiet in there."

"It usually is," Gertie said with a cryptic smile. "Well" —she stuck out her hand— "good luck!"

Emily shook the girl's hand. "Thank you, Gertie. I am certain I shall bump along just fine."

"It's the bumps I'm worried about, miss." The little maid nodded in the direction of the nursery, winked, and left.

As Emily put on her shawl and stockings and shoes, she thought about what she'd learned of the Viscount Winter. The more his parents had tightened their hold on him, the more he'd struggled. Eventually, he'd bucked and reared and wildly galloped off toward Ruination.

She thought about the austere nursery. Was he now doing the same thing to his own children?

A peek into the nursery told her they were still intently busy, one curled up with a book on the window seat, and another happily playing with her doll amongst a riot of wood blocks. Emily smiled. There was nothing to being a governess. It was easy. All one had to do was understand children, and Emily had several younger cousins.

Gathering her shawl about her, she stole past the children and out the nursery door on her way to the stables. It would take only a few moments to explain the situation to Mr. Sneed, the stable master. She'd be gone no more than five minutes. All would be well.

Down at the stables, Mr. Sneed was pretending to be hard at work on a new harness, but Emily saw that he had moved his worktable to the far end of the barn, next to the stall where the baby elephant was hidden, and that he wasn't looking at the harness at all, but into the stall, a wide grin on his face.

"Hullo!" he called when he saw Emily approach.

"You've been away a while. Must have had a grand meal!"

"Indeed," she replied with a smile, and she explained about her new position as temporary governess. "And so," she concluded, "if it pleases you, I will accept the position formally the next time I see the Viscount."

"You ain't already accepted the position?"

She looked cautiously about them.

"There ain't no one around to hear us," the old man said, guessing her concern. "I set the lot of 'em to other tasks."

She nodded. "I needed to speak with you first, for I cannot be the children's governess and the elephant's caretaker all at once. I shall have to ask you to care for her until Miss Bull returns and I leave here."

"Where will you go? What will you do with *her*?" He hooked a thumb toward the elephant.

She bit her lip. "I do not know," she admitted. "I thought I might find a way to send her back to India or Ceylon. Or perhaps I will discover another menagerie or circus that will take her."

"Aw ... no, miss! Not another menagerie! What makes you fancy the next will treat that little baby any better than the last one did? You just can't!"

"She *is* an elephant, Mr. Sneed. I spent everything I had to acquire her, and now I cannot afford to feed her, much less to send her back to her probable birthplace. But if I cannot, then I will not have a choice. I can hardly keep her in—" She'd almost said 'London!' "I can hardly keep her in your barn forever. Which brings me to another matter. If your master discovers her here without his permission—"

"Now, don't you worry none about that. He's not going to find out about it, busy as he is just now."

"Unless I tell him."

"Tell him?" A little-girl voice cried from behind her. "You mustn't tell him!"

"Rose!" Emily whirled around. "Go back to the nursery at once!"

"But we already know about the elephant."

"We were listening," Rain explained helpfully. "May we see the baby?"

"Please?" Rose pleaded

"Yes, please?"

Emily put her hand to her suddenly pounding forehead. "Now I *must* tell him!"

"No, you don't," Mr. Sneed said. "If you're worried about Wild and Willful here spilling the beans, think no more on it. Little as they are, they know how to keep secrets."

"You mustn't tell him," Rose said. "Papa will be upset. Baby elephants are fun—at least I fancy they are, since you haven't even let me see one, yet!" She glared. "And Papa doesn't like fun."

"He'd be cross," Rain agreed.

"They're right," Mr. Sneed said. "If you tell him, he'll be vexed—especially now, during his house party. Why trouble him with it? I'll be up in the boughs happy to keep our little baby out here in the barn. And if his lordship discovers she's here ... why, you can cross that bridge when you come to it. What can he do, dismiss you?"

"No, but he *could* dismiss *you*."

The old man smiled. "He could, but he won't. This ain't the first time I kept something hidden in my barn. The master ain't always been such a high stickler, an' I used to keep secrets for him when he was a lad. Brought me everything from baby ducks to hedgehogs. One time, he brought home a fox he'd rescued from his father's hunt!" His blue eyes twinkled. "No, he won't be dismissing old Mr. Sneed. Best not tell."

Emily considered a moment, while three sets of

eyes silently implored her. She sighed. "You know him better than I. Very well. I shall not tell him."

All three gave a joyful *whoop*.

Mr. Sneed patted Emily's head as though she were a child. "Let's go in and see our baby."

4

FANCY FRIPPERY

*T*HE NEXT DAY dawned clear and fine, and Emily spent much of it outside with her charges, exploring—something they hadn't been allowed to do before. Emily let them choose where to go and simply followed, enjoying their delighted shrieks and giggles of discovery. They cavorted with Sir Basil's dogs and splashed their feet in the icy brook. With no flowers available, Emily showed them how to make daisy chains using ivy, and both children wore their green crowns throughout the day.

Emily had decided they would take luncheon right in the middle of the lively Stendmore Park kitchen. The girls spent entirely too much time cooped up in that stuffy old nursery. But just as they walked though the back door, both girls whipped their crowns from their head and dropped them into one of the large flowerpots that flanked the door.

"You can wear them inside," Emily assured them, bending to pick up the crowns.

"No!" Rose said. "Papa wouldn't like it."

"Why not?" Emily asked. "Your crowns are lovely."

Rain's little face bunched up. "We never show Papa nonsensical things." She turned to follow her sister into the kitchen.

"Well, *I* do not think they are nonsensical," Emily declared, snatching the crowns from the flowerpot. Back inside, she placed them on the girls' heads, so that everyone in the kitchen could admire them, and admire them they did—vocally, and with much enthusiasm.

Eating lunch in the kitchen seemed to delight the girls, and it certainly delighted Emily. Meals in her parents' house were always staid affairs, but the kitchen table at Stendmore Park was full of people laughing and chatting, and Emily had never attended such a lively and pleasant meal. It was good to be a governess!

Cook spoke to Emily when she went to refill her own teacup. "It was fine to see the little moppets outside on a beautiful day like today. Miss Bull keeps them inside most of the time, and they never get to run around making crowns and such." She smiled at the girls. "And they ain't misbehaving at all! You must have run all the steam out of them."

"No, no," Emily protested, "they just need somewhere to focus their energy. I have younger cousins," she confided.

"Well, good for you, I say. I was sure when his lordship hired you yesterday, you'd be eaten alive." She chuckled. "I'm that glad to see you're in one piece."

"Thank you," Emily smiled. "I shall endeavor to keep me that way."

Though she would have wished otherwise, luncheon did not last long. More guests had arrived, and the kitchen was a hive of activity. Emily and the children helped by getting out of the way.

Three-o'-the-clock found them outside in the barren winter garden, skipping colored stones across the small, reflecting pond there and listening to Emily tell stories.

She had discovered they were fascinated with anything having to do with Christmas, which, up until now, had been all but ignored at Stendmore Park.

When the staff had seen the crowns of green upon the girls' heads, they had remarked that Lord Winter had ordered the house to be filled with green stuff on Christmas Eve, six days hence. The staff seemed delighted at the prospect and already pots and pots of fragrant fir, ivy, holly, bay, and rosemary stood at the ready, which puzzled the girls, who had never seen Christmas greenery brought inside before.

"Why can we not bring the green stuff inside now? Let us hang it right now. Today. Please?" Rose begged.

"Not yet. It is considered unlucky to bring the greenery into the house before Christmas Eve," Emily answered.

"Do you fancy Papa will eat some of the Christmas pudding?" Rain asked dreamily.

"He did order it himself," Emily said, though she'd wondered at the same thing. If the apple didn't fall far from the tree, then why was Lord Winter making plans to celebrate Christmas so lavishly? She'd seen yesterday that he didn't even know what sort of dishes were traditionally served at Christmastime. What had changed his mind?

She supposed it was the house party.

"Papa has been awfully cross ever since he

decided to have the house party," Rose said skeptically. "Maybe he won't let *us* have any pudding."

"Yes, maybe it's only for the guests," Rain speculated gloomily.

"Yes," Rose said, "Grandmama and Grandpapa didn't like Christmas at all. They called it 'fancy frippery'" —she lowered her voice and looked around— "and the servants say he's just like them."

"Nonsense," Emily said. "If he is just like them, then why is he holding the house party at all? Did your grandparents ever hold house parties?"

Both girls shook their heads.

"Well, then. Since this is the first Christmas you have spent with your father, perhaps you should not be so quick to foretell doom. Heavens, you shall probably have two portions of pudding, for the servants will be having their own down in the servants' hall, and I am right and tight you shall be welcome to some of that. In fact, I know of a certain governess who will make sure of it. And you shall have other things as well: Christmas pie and—"

Rain's eyes grew big. "Christmas pie? What is that?"

Emily smiled. "It is delicious, that's what it is."

"What else will there be?" Rose asked, and

Emily went through a catalog of all the traditional dishes. "… and there will be a Yule log, and we shall hang greenery on Christmas Eve and play games and sing and—oh, girls, you shall have a wonderful time!"

They talked about it in minute detail for the next hour. The sisters were pitifully excited about a simple Yule log. They'd never had one. They were delighted when Emily told them that the Christmas pudding would have special favors inside. And the idea of mistletoe and stolen kisses had them giggling and rolling on the grass.

Emily let them be.

Though she had known them only for a day, she was certain she understood them. They were rebellious simply because they'd been under such strict control all their lives. No Yule log, no green stuff, not even so much as a plum pudding! These poor children had been deprived. If they were treated that way at Christmas, she shuddered to think how the rest of the year must have gone.

Well, Christmas was only a week away, and Miss Bull was unlikely to return before then, so Emily had a chance to correct past injustices for the girls this Christmas.

And she'd decided something else, as well.

She'd thought that once this adventure was over, she would never find herself playing the part of governess again. But the past day had been so pleasant that an idea had crept into her mind: she could be a governess for as long as she wanted—or needed—to be. But first, she'd have to ask Lord Winter for a reference, and that meant that she had to do a good job. She was going to have to teach the girls *something*, yet she was certain that if she marched them up to the schoolroom, they would be vastly resistant to the idea.

Therefore, she would begin to teach them right here where they were, outside, and she'd let marching up to the schoolroom be their idea. It was a brilliant plan, and she smiled in anticipated triumph.

Being a governess was easy. Everything was going to be fine.

Emily gathered them close atop her large shawl, and they all basked in the sunshine as Emily told them an old story she'd heard from her nurse, years and years before. It was a great favorite of hers, one she loved to tell her little cousins. And, like her cousins, Rose and Rain listened raptly.

"And so," Emily ended the story, "just at the

stroke of midnight on Christmas Eve, if you listen closely, you can hear the animals talk."

"What do they say?" Rose asked in wonder.

"Oh," Emily answered, "anything that comes to their minds."

"Have *you* ever heard them speak?"

Emily smiled, for she'd been waiting for that question. "Of course I have."

"What did they say to you?" Rain asked, her eyes full of curiosity.

"Yes, yes! What did they say?"

"I will tell you," Emily said, "after you tell me."

They threw her questioning looks. "What do you mean?" Rain asked.

"I mean that I have been telling you stories all day, and you have told me none in return. I wish to hear a story. I want you to tell me the story of *What the Animals Said to Miss Jones*. But you must write your stories down before sharing them. You will write them down in English, Rain, while you, Rose, will write them down in French. And when you are finished, you will read them to the staff."

"In the servants' hall?" Rain asked.

"Can I read mine to the servants myself?" Rose's eyes were shining.

A voice sliced through the air just behind them. "No. No, you most certainly cannot!"

Emily spun around and her eyes opened wide. It was the Viscount, and unlike yesterday, he was dressed in the first stare of fashion. A bottle green coat over an embroidered waistcoat; tight, buff-colored inexpressibles; top boots with a mirror-shine; snowy-white linen cravat and high shirt points. Amongst the folds of his cravat winked a modest emerald. All of the finest quality.

Someone had cut his dark, glossy curls, and if it didn't quite fit the mould of a Brutus haircut, it certainly didn't hurt his image. His windswept, slightly longer-than-normal hair made him look a little wild, as though he had just stepped off some lonely moor and into the hearts of lonely women everywhere. Why, he wouldn't have looked out of place in St. James's Street or Hyde Park on a Sunday afternoon. He was stunning.

She blinked. He was also angry.

David frowned as his daughters scrambled to stand and Miss Jones gathered her skirts with one hand

and held out her other. "I was just telling the story of the animals talking on—"

"Yes. I heard," he said, helping her to her feet. Her hand was small in his. "Why?"

"Run along, children," she directed his daughters. "Go play down by the pond. Go practice skipping stones as I showed you earlier."

She turned to face David. He hadn't realized how short of stature she was. The top of her head barely reached his shoulder. "I told you," she said evenly. "I am teaching the children. What does it look like I am doing?"

David almost smiled. She was bold and spirited, qualities he admired, but they would not help her in her capacity as a servant—for that is what she was now, no matter what her status in her former life had been. She'd probably have no choice other than to remain a governess—and a bold and spirited governess was not The Thing. Under other circumstances, those same qualities would have helped her cut a fine dash in the ballrooms of London. But in the vast majority of households they would get her dismissed. For her own sake, he needed to make her understand that before she left Stendmore Park.

He pasted on a frown. "Teaching them? Why?"

"I am their governess," she answered.

"Only temporarily," he said. "I do not expect you to perform the duties of a true governess. I expect you to be more of a ... a keeper."

"Ah ..." She nodded. "I see. Like ... the keeper of a lion, an ape, or—"

"Or any other wild animal you can name. Yes."

A smile burst forth upon her face, and David was struck by the sudden beauty of it. Her brown eyes seemed to shine with a merry light all their own, and he found himself smiling back in spite of his irritation.

"I know what your expectations are, but I hope you will not mind if I attempt to conduct myself as a proper governess would. If I perform my duties well, you may be willing to give me a reference for a similar position elsewhere."

David smiled again. "Are you always so bold?" he asked.

"I am. Does that displease you?"

"On the contrary. I prefer it." And he did. "Some people would call such plain speaking a virtue, Miss Jones. If more people asked and answered questions truthfully, much strife would be avoided in this world."

She held his gaze as he thought about her

request. He could see no harm in it. She was clearly an intelligent lady of good breeding—and he had to admit that he was pleased with her performance thus far. An entire day had gone by without disaster.

"Carry on," he said and turned to go. "Although," he paused, "a proper governess would focus the attention of her charges upon their lessons, not upon play. Upon reality, rather than upon fantasy. Especially these children. I know them well, and it takes little provocation for them to plunge into abandon."

"Abandon?" she asked, her expression bemused.

"My daughters are infamous for their rambunctious behavior."

"Do you mean that they are playful?"

"Call it what you will."

Suddenly, inexplicably, her face folded into an expression of annoyance. "You seem to equate playfulness with evil, my lord. They are children. They need to play."

David flicked a glance over at the Hellions. They weren't playing as she'd directed them to but standing still, staring at them from a distance. They were probably trying to catch a word on the breeze or read lips. "It seems to me they have had quite enough play for one day."

"It seems to me they have had too little."

"They are my children," he countered, "and they need to learn responsibility. Miss Jones, are you aware that everyone within five miles of Stendmore Park calls my children Wild and Willful instead of Rose and Rain?"

It was true. David had discovered that fact a few days after he'd come home, and he'd been amused, even prideful—until he'd heard the whispers: *'Wild and Willful—just like their father. No good will come of them.'*

He hadn't paid much mind to such talk at first, but the seeds were sown, and David had begun to think about them. While his parents were alive, Stendmore Park had prospered, but under his brother's care, it had withered and all but died. Six months of David's labor from sunup to sundown hadn't been able to bring it back to life. He hadn't the knowledge. And why? Because he'd hied off to London before he could learn any of it. Now he needed to hire a steward to help him and couldn't. And why? Because he didn't have enough money. And he didn't have enough money because he'd been undisciplined and irresponsible. He'd squandered the legacy left him by his grandfather and neglected the estate as his brother had drunk it all away.

It was David's fault. All of it was his fault.

If he'd been home instead of in the gaming hells or his mistress's arms or on a blasted ship, his little girls would already be able to control the wild impulses they'd inherited from him. God knew they hadn't received any bad qualities from their poor, timid mother.

Though he hadn't loved her, he had admired her goodness, and he'd been sad when he'd heard she was gone.

He blinked once, twice, and, finding his attention had wandered, raked his hand through his hair. "See here," he told Miss Jones. "My daughters need correction. They need control. You must not encourage their wildness. I have seen you roving about the countryside all day long. You ought to be giving them lessons," he said.

"I was until you interrupted us."

"You were telling them fairy stories. I heard you."

"I was telling them the story of the animals talking on Christmas Eve."

David cut the air with one hand. "It is fiction."

"You know that, and I know that, but they do not."

"Precisely. They believe you, which only proves my point. You should not be encouraging them to indulge in fantasy."

She put one hand on her hip and gestured with the other. "People cannot do things unless they imagine them first, my lord. It seems to me that one of the responsibilities of a good governess is to develop her charges' imaginations. Your children need to exercise their imaginations more, not less."

"Do you realize how impertinent you are being?"

"Impertinent, my lord? Or merely possessing a different opinion?"

He couldn't believe this conversation was happening. "Are you always this way? So incautious?"

"I do not understand."

"Of course not!" He blew air up through his hair. "Miss Jones, you leap into the air when there is no net, trusting that it will appear."

Another dazzling smile blossomed on her face. "Yes. Exactly! You are right." She seemed proud of it. "*Carpe diem*. Seize the day!"

She just didn't understand. "Sometimes, Miss

Jones, the net does not appear. Sooner or later, you will jump to your death."

"Better that than die of boredom," she countered.

The dratted errant curl that refused to stay fell over his brow, and David raked it back into place yet again. "Miss Jones, there are other ways to drill them in French without having them concoct some outrageous stories. I believe there are French books in the nursery."

"There *are* French books," she said. "*Boring* French books. And they are probably old enough to have bored *you* to tears, my lord. If a governess wants her charges to apply themselves, she must make the lessons interesting."

He sighed. He was getting nowhere, and he was beginning to doubt he ever would. She was a stubborn woman. Almost as stubborn as he was. "I bow to your great experience and authority," he said, walking away. "I shall be pleased to extol the results of your pedagogy in your letter of reference." He meant his tone to be sarcastic, but somehow it came out sounding amused instead.

Emily watched him go, the sun glinting off his dazzlingly white cravat and his shiny brown hair. He was carefully dressed today, his bearing stiff and formal. But that hair! It would not be tamed. Tall and broad of shoulder, he was a strikingly handsome man with wide-set, intelligent blue eyes and a frank countenance. But as they'd spoken, she'd noticed something about him that didn't seem to fit. Deep lines in his face. Laugh lines. Dimples. He must smile often.

Yet she'd hardly seen him smile since she'd arrived.

Emily turned to the children and held out her hand. They came to her at once.

"Don't mind Papa," Rose told her, accurately guessing her father's state of mind. "He has been cross for a fortnight—ever since he decided to hold the house party."

"Well, if the mere thought of holding a house party makes him cross, I wonder why he decided to have one at all?" Emily mused aloud.

Rain gave her skirt a little tug. "Can we go visit the elephant? Please?"

Emily wasn't certain that was a good idea. What if Lord Winter should see them heading for the barn and decide to follow them? Yesterday, she'd merely thought he'd be annoyed. Today, she was absolutely certain he would explode like a firework. "I fancy that is not a good idea," Emily said. "Not right now. What about your stories?"

"We can do them later," Rain offered.

"We could go to the barn later, too," Emily said.

"It will be dark later," Rose said, "and much colder. You wouldn't take us out in the cold, would you?"

"An' in the dark," Rain said, her face serious.

"Yes," Rose said. "Rain is afraid of the dark. She has nightmares ..." The girl's voice trailed off, and Emily was suddenly alert, though she was uncertain why she should be. She did not have to wait long to find out, however, for Rose said after a moment, "I have nightmares, too."

"Oh?"

"Yes. And ... I talk in my sleep."

"I see,"

"And sometimes I mention things I should not."

"Mmm."

"Like wanting to see elephants," she said, her face tilting up toward Emily and one eyebrow rising high on her forehead.

It was a threat. Rose was trying to blackmail her governess!

"Oh, dear!" Emily said carefully and walked on, considering what she should do. She a little reassured to discover there was some truth behind their nicknames. She'd met strictly obedient children, and they always made her uneasy. It was as if something were missing in them somehow. But Rose and Rain were normal, happy little girls—or they would be if only they were allowed to play more.

"I believe I have changed my mind, ladies," she said after a moment. "I suppose it would do no harm to visit the elephant, as long as we are careful about how and when we approach the barn."

As Emily thought it would, Rose's face registered surprise. She hadn't expected her gambit to work. Like a bulldog who has chased a cat for years only to discover he does not know what to do with her when he finally catches her, Rose was unsure of herself. Her steps faltered and slowed as emotion marched across her face. Satisfaction, then worry, then guilt. Inside, Emily smiled and walked on, chattering with Rain about the possibility of Christmas snow.

"Miss Emily?" the voice from behind them came at last.

"Yes, Rose?"

"I didn't mean it."

"I know, dearling. But then, neither did I. We are still going to the schoolroom—after a short visit to the stables."

Beside her, Rose said nothing, but after a moment, she giggled and placed her hand in Emily's. Emily's fingers closed around the little girl's, Rain joined them on her other side, and off they went to the stable yard.

When at last the elephant saw the children, she ran around her stall excitedly throwing straw into the air with her short little trunk. Emily laughed. "It looks like she is vastly enthusiastic this afternoon."

"Yes," said Mr. Sneed, "she's happy to see the girls again."

A sly look passed between the sisters, and again Emily was instantly alert.

Heedless of the dynamic, Mr. Sneed chuckled. "I'll wager she wants more syllabub."

"Syllabub?" Emily asked. "*More* syllabub?"

The girls were suddenly terribly interested in their frocks, the manger, the door lock, their hair—anything to avoid Emily's gaze.

"She loves it so," said Mr. Sneed. "Fortunately, there's plenty to go around." He hooked his thumb toward a crock stationed just outside the stall door. "Cook can't get the recipe right. New to the job," he added. "But Baby don't mind."

"She likes it," Rain said, unable to keep still any longer. "She tossed it about just like the straw at first, but then she tasted it, and—"

"And it seemed a shame to let it go to waste," Rose said, discerning the secret obviously had been exposed.

"And I couldn't see much harm in it," the stable master said. "It don't have much wine in it, and seeing as she's so big and it's cold out, and she loves it so, I judged it fine."

"Obviously," Emily said, eyeing Baby's eagerly questing trunk and roving eyes, and then she gave the girls a stern look. "And you named her 'Baby' last night, I presume? In the middle of the night, when everyone else was asleep?"

The girls lowered their eyes to the floor. "Yes, miss," they said in unison.

Mr. Sneed scowled. "I thought you'd given your permission for them to visit the stables, miss."

Emily sighed. "Ladies, you must not do that again. It is dangerous for little girls to be up wandering about at night, and I do not want you to be hurt. If I find you've done it again, I will have to punish you for it. Do you understand?"

"You are not going to punish us this time?" Rose asked, incredulous.

Emily shook her head. "I cannot punish you for a rule I have not set down, now can I?"

"Well, you could," Mr. Sneed said, "but I'd have wagered you wouldn't." He smiled broadly at her and patted her hand as he nudged open the stall door.

The girls pushed inside, and Baby met them eagerly, her questing little trunk exploring their hair, their dresses, their shoe buttons, their ribbons—one of which she promptly purloined and ran about waving excitedly. The girls promptly gave chase, and all three had a grand time.

When they tired of that game, with her sister's help, Rain tied her bonnet onto Baby's head, the top of which was about equal in height with her own. Baby was surprisingly agile and quick for her size, and Emily was a little worried at first that she might knock the girls over or step on them, but Baby was also amazingly gentle.

In fact, Baby was a little lady—a little lady who would not remain little, Emily reminded herself.

"Baby" was an appropriate name for her now, but someday it would seem comical. Nevertheless, Emily shrugged off the thought with her usual optimism. No need to worry about it. Everything would work out well in the end. It always did.

5

A CAGED LION

*D*AVID THREW DOWN his fourth ruined cravat and cursed into the looking glass. He'd nicked himself whilst shaving, one button was a little loose, and he'd tried to coax his hair into a devilishly fashionable Brutus look but ended up simply looking like the devil.

He looked like the scapegrace he was, he supposed. How was he to convince his guests he'd changed, looking like this?

There was only one more pressed cravat left. In the absence of a properly trained valet, David would have to iron them all himself later, after tonight's dinner party. But then, after tonight's dinner party, he might not have any need for pressed cravats or

Brutus haircuts. It wouldn't matter what he looked like, if he couldn't behave respectably.

He certainly hadn't behaved respectably this afternoon.

What had come over him? Berating Miss Jones for being a bloody poor governess made no bloody sense. She *wasn't* a governess, so what had he expected?

He hadn't expected to be surprised. Alarmed. And … and *charmed*, that's what. When she'd taken him to task for a lack of whimsy, he'd been angry, at first. There she was, obviously destitute and utterly dependent upon his good opinion of her, lecturing him on the proper way to educate his children. And then … well, as he'd stood there looking down at Miss Jones puffing up like a Banty hen, he'd had to beat down a sudden laugh. She was fearless, unflinching, presumptuous and … and utterly adorable.

Was she also right? Was he being too harsh, expecting too much of his children?

He swore again.

He'd been outside, looking to escape his forced captivity for a moment. He'd felt like a lion at a menagerie all day. His guests were watching him, waiting for him to rage and roar. Especially Mrs. Kellerman, the old biddy.

David detested Mrs. Kellerman.

When he was a boy, he'd sneaked into the Kellerman's stables at dusk to catch a glimpse of a pair of twin foals, newly born, only to find one of them hanging by its leg from its mother's halter. Somehow the poor thing had become entangled, and the stable master was nowhere to be seen. The entire staff was at their evening meal, which was why David had been able to sneak into the stable in the first place.

David was but five or six years old, but one look at the dam's wild eyes and he'd known right away that both foals and mother were in mortal danger.

He'd run into the house, screaming for help, overshooting the entrance to the servants' hall and running straight into the Kellerman's grand dining room instead—where they were currently entertaining the parson and his wife, who sat staring at David as though he'd sprouted tentacles from his ears.

David tried to explain what was happening in the stable, but by that time he was nearly hysterical, and no one listened. Mrs. Kellerman ordered him taken outside, and a footman grabbed David by the collar. Which was why David grabbed for the first solid thing his hands came in contact with—which happened to be Mrs. Kellerman's long, pearl necklace.

The footman jerked his arm, the necklace snapped, pearls flew through the air, and one of them landed in Mrs. Kellerman's open mouth. And then, to David's utter surprise—and to Mrs. Kellerman's, judging by the look on her face, she swallowed it, with one great, loud *gulp*.

The parson's wife, bless her, giggled.

The footman, no-doubt seeing murder in his mistress's eyes, hustled David out the door and down the hall, where the staff, alerted by the commotion, were crowded. David babbled out his story, and the stable master and his boys ran outside with poor little David in their wake.

The horse and foals were saved, but the stable master rang a peal over David and boxed his ears nonetheless, and he got a second scolding the next morning from his parents *and* no supper that evening—a punishment suggested by Mrs. Kellerman, who told him so with a satisfied smile the next Sunday at church.

He'd hated her ever since. Her and her ilk.

Except for Sir Basil and his wife, Lady Griselda,

no one had ever taken an interest in what David said. Over the years, the old couple sometimes appeared at the Buxley Assembly, which David had often sneaked out to attend when he was a youngster. Once, when he was about twelve, they'd given him a ride home in Sir Basil's traveling carriage during a rainstorm. They'd fed him cold roast chicken, seed cake, and lemonade they'd packed for their return trip home. Then they quizzed him endlessly about his parents and Robert.

They'd gone out of their way to be good to him after that.

But, as kind as Sir Basil and Lady Griselda were, they were not relatives, and they lived over in Alderly, two leagues' distance from Buxley-on-Isis. Only rarely did David see them. His own parents did not entertain.

David's was a lonely upbringing. He was the second son. The extra. The superfluous. The unneeded. And everyone knew he'd be shipped off to Northumberland or some such place as soon as he reached his majority.

No matter how hard David tried to be good, to excel at his studies, to be respectful, helpful, cheerful, no one ever listened to him, apart from Sir Basil and Lady Griselda.

They listened to David's older brother, though. They invited Robert to picnics. They introduced him to their young daughters. They fawned over him.

Always in Robert's shadow, David was barely even noticed.

At some point—David could not now say exactly when it was—he decided to *make* them notice. All of them. And since he couldn't seem do it by way of being good, he'd had no choice but to do so by being bad.

And David found was very, very good at being bad.

For years, he'd delighted in making gulping noises whenever he saw Mrs. Kellerman and, in case she didn't catch his meaning (she did), he enquired sweetly as to whether or not she'd had her pearls fixed yet (she had not).

Mrs. Kellerman never wore pearls again.

He almost wished he hadn't invited her to the house party, but she and her husband were the richest people in the neighborhood. Inviting her had been a necessary evil.

His daughters' futures hung by a thread. He couldn't let them fall, and—blast it all!—all was dependent upon Mrs. Kellerman and the rest. He hated being at their mercy. He hated not being in control. And worst of all he hated that his little girls were dependent upon them, too.

So far, by some miracle, Miss Jones had managed to keep Rose and Rain out of trouble and away from his guests, as he'd asked her to. But she'd also been roaming over the grounds with them and allowing them to eat in the kitchen with the servants.

If she didn't keep them hidden away, sooner or later they'd be found by one of his guests. They'd be scrutinized and inspected as closely as David was. And they'd be found lacking. Perhaps he should order Miss Jones to keep them in the nursery for the entire house party.

No.

He rejected the idea as soon as it occurred. In his long absence, the neighborhood had already judged Rose and Rain. They thought them "wild and willful," and it was no use trying to convincing them otherwise. His daughters were children, and their behavior would eventually be overlooked, as long as David exhibited rock-solid respectability.

He'd wager his last groat that the unflinching Miss Jones wouldn't follow such an order anyway. And then he would have to sack her. Or marry her.

He snorted. Absurd idea.

He comforted himself with the thought that she'd been doing a good job with the girls. His staff had reported that she'd worked some sort of miracle on them. But David knew better. They would revert as soon as Miss Jones's newness wore off. He was all too familiar with the headstrong, undisciplined defiance that ran in their blood. Once he'd had a taste of it, he'd been unstoppable.

But he'd had no one to love him. Even Miss Bull had been preoccupied with David's elder brother. She'd been affectionate—to a point.

He didn't want his girls to have that same sort of upbringing. David made an effort to visit the nursery each night before they went to sleep. No matter how busy he was, he took the time to make sure they knew he cared. He didn't tell them any silly bedtime fairy stories, of course, but he asked them about their studies and told them he loved them. They were good little girls, and David did love them. Dearly.

Which was why he had to convince everyone he'd changed. And he had, by Jove! Otherwise, he couldn't have stood people poking about his house, peering into his study, questioning his servants. But Mrs. Kellerman was the worst of the lot. Poring over Stendmore Park as though it were her property. His new housekeeper had reported that she'd found Mrs. Kellerman inspecting the china, his new butler said "the old harpy, beggin' your pardon, my lord" had been admonishing him for the way he decanted wine, and David had actually caught her running a white glove over the mantelpiece, checking for dust!

But through it all, he'd held his bloody temper — until today, when Miss Jones had provoked him.

Her behavior was beyond impertinent. She'd been outrageously pert. But that was no reason for David to act ungentlemanly. Ungentlemanly hell! He'd been positively beastly. And poor Miss Jones was the person at Stendmore Park who *least* deserved it.

David swore.

It wasn't like him to berate servants. Or pretty young ladies.

He swore again and snatched up his last good cravat.

He was certain he'd never seen Miss Jones in London — he could never have overlooked a beauty like that — so he guessed she was gentry. She was no-doubt the daughter of some rich landowner or other, though she could also be a rector's offspring, he supposed. Folding the cravat lengthwise once, twice, he draped it over his neck. While David did not know her exact circumstances, he did know Miss Jones had come down in the world—and recently, judging by the fashionable cut of the dress she'd arrived in. Recent impoverishment could only mean one thing: she'd lost her protector—a father or husband—and she obviously had no one else.

No one but David.

What was he going to do with her when Miss Bull returned? He could hardly turn her out. He'd have to find some sort of position for her. Estates had under gardeners. Did they have under-governesses? As he smoothed one fold of the cravat, it suddenly occurred to David that, with an aging, ailing mother to care for, Miss Bull might not return at all. If that happened, David would have to pension her off—and find a permanent replacement.

Emily Jones might do nicely—if David could manage to ignore a beautiful, gently-bred young woman who was living right in his blasted house. He couldn't show her any deference at all. He could only imagine what Mrs. Kellerman would say if she got wind of him sniffing around his children's governess!

It suddenly occurred to him that Miss Jones

might not welcome such attentions anyway. In fact, she probably would not. She was a gently-bred young lady, after all. She wouldn't think the attentions of her employer were proper any more than Mrs. Kellerman would. And neither did he!

He yanked at the corner of the cravat a little too hard and grunted.

He needed to stop thinking about Miss Jones. He had more important matters to consider than governesses, he told himself, but then he sighed and stared at his reflection. "You are a widower," he muttered. "A poor widower with two little girls to care for. A widower *viscount* with no money to support your title or estate or those little girls." He sighed.

He needed a governess for his children and an heiress for himself.

An heiress.

Oh yes, the idea had been stalking him for some time. It was inescapable. A wealthy heiress with a desire to trade her fortune for a title was just the thing to lift David out of his current financial predicament. And London teemed with them every Season, but David wasn't a duke or a marquess or even an earl. He was just a viscount and an impoverished one to boot. Desirable enough for women in their third, fourth, or fifth season who hadn't yet been able to snare a titled husband in spite of their wealth. They were always a miserable lot. Shrewish, stupid, or both.

David shuddered. He didn't want to be shackled to someone he could not respect. He needed to find someone he could love. Someone sweet. Someone clever and bold.

An image of Miss Jones sprang to mind, and he gave his cravat a savage twist.

What he needed was a new cravat.

David stared into the cheval glass at the hopelessly mangled jumble of fine, white linen and sighed. He needed to look and act respectable so he could beg a loan from his neighbors and secure his daughter's futures. But first, he needed to forget about Miss Jones.

No matter how deserving she was.

Or how sad her story.

Or how pretty she was …with her brown hair shining in the sunlight … and her lovely, dark eyes glinting with indignation …

David growled in frustration and, after hastily retying his last, ruined cravat as best he could, departed for the drawing room.

Back into the lion's cage he went.

6

THE MATCHMAKER

*A*S HER CHARGES worked on their stories later that day, Emily stepped out of the nursery and walked along the hall to ease her legs—and her mind.

She was the type of person who needed a measure of solitude each day in order to function properly, even if it were only a few stolen moments. She didn't intend to go far, just down the corridor a short distance and back. She would avoid the public rooms entirely, keeping to this floor, which was reserved for the children and the servants' quarters. All the guests would be downstairs playing at cards or billiards, embroidering, or just plain gossiping.

And so it was that Emily was surprised to see the Viscount coming toward her down the hall.

"Miss Jones," he said with a bow. "Where are the children?" He glanced behind her.

"They are working on their lessons," she said, neglecting to tell him that they were writing down their stories."

"I suppose that whichever poor soul you have left them with is suitably armed?" He crooked an eyebrow.

"Mmm," Emily averred, mirroring his expression, and said nothing more. The girls *were* alone in the nursery, but she'd promised that if they behaved while she was away, they would be allowed access to her wardrobe upon her return. They knew she'd been given the clothes that belonged to their mother. Neither of them had any memory of her, and they were eager to explore the gowns and fripperies. Emily had even promised they could try them on. So she was one hundred percent certain there would be no mischief from either of them while she strolled the halls. But the Viscount—a man!—would not understand that.

"Miss Jones. I ... uh ..." He shifted uncomfortably. "I find myself in the position of having to apologize. I was sharp with you today, and" —He cleared his throat— "If I wish for you to modify what you teach my children, I should tell you so, not shout. I was most … uncivil. Please forgive me." The Viscount stuck out his hand for Emily to shake.

She took his hand automatically. It was warm and soft and hard and silky. Electricity seemed to spark down her spine when they touched, and an emptiness settled over her when, by mutual consent, they withdrew their hands. He folded his arm behind his back, as though he felt it too, but Emily told herself she was being silly. She was simply inexperienced with men, that was all. He was no more interested in her than Sir Basil was!

He went on. "While I still disagree with your choice of lessons, I must admit that your presence has been nothing short of a godsend."

He smiled suddenly, a dimple appearing at the corner of his generous mouth, his teeth white and even, his blue eyes sparkling, and Emily could have sworn she saw the sun shine into the dimly lit, windowless hallway.

"Though inexperienced, Miss Jones, you are apparently good with children, as there has not been one *crash*, *bang*, or *boom* from the nursery since you arrived. No ropes have been lowered from upstairs windows, and the Hellions haven't once been seen downstairs. I commend you."

"The Hellions?"

"My pet name for them," he said. "Do not worry. It is but a joke between us. I would never call them that in front of … an outsider. I am not always an overbearing curmudgeon, as I was earlier."

She felt herself blush. "I am indeed glad to hear it, my lord."

"I wish to make it up to you," he said, tucking her arm into his. "Come. Let us walk together. I presume you are taking a short break from the Hellions? That is just the thing." He pulled her down the hall.

So, Emily thought to herself, *Lord Winter isn't made of ice after all!* No … on the contrary, his arm felt quite warm—and so did Emily's face. She wasn't used to being in this close proximity to men, she supposed. Especially handsome young men who looked at her the way the Viscount was looking at her right then!

"You look charming today," he said, as they walked. "That gown suits you."

"Thank you for lending it to me," she said. "It was most kind of you."

"I have no use for those clothes. You may keep them, if you wish."

"Thank you," she said, "but are you certain? You

would look lovely swirling about the floor in them at Almack's!"

He laughed aloud, a lovely, surprising sound. "Ah, Almack's. A dreadfully dull and boring place, don't you think?"

"I ... would not know," Emily said. "I have never been." It was true. Almack's Assembly Rooms were widely known as the showcase of the *ton's* marriage mart, and she'd steadfastly refused to attend.

"Trust me," he said, "it is not all they claim. It is rather drab and the refreshments sub-par. The cake is stale and the lemonade watered down."

"Oh dear, stale cake!" She laughed. "A travesty indeed."

They chatted amiably as they strolled the hallway. Emily was so absorbed in their conversation that they were halfway down the stairs before she realized they were on them.

"I—I must go back to the nursery," she stammered.

"Why? The children are fine with whomever you left in charge. My staff knows not to let them out of their sight." He smiled easily. "You must come with me."

"Why?"

He gave her a kind smile. "Many of my guests have younger sons," he said cryptically.

"I beg your pardon?"

"No," he said, "it is I who should be begging yours, for what I am about to say. Pray forgive me, Miss Jones, but I must speak freely."

"I give you leave," she said.

He sketched a bow. "See here …" He hesitated, and Emily knew that whatever he was about to say was awkward for him. He plunged on: "It has not escaped my notice that you must have come down in the world, for you are clearly a well brought up young lady, and I find I cannot in all good conscience dine in company downstairs today without inviting you to join us. Pray come downstairs with me. It is nearly teatime."

"Oh!" Emily panicked, knowing she could not do as he suggested without being recognized. "Oh. I …"

At that moment, she was saved from having to find a plausible excuse by the appearance of Sir Basil and Lady Griselda.

"Well, well!" Sir Basil smiled. "Who do we have here?"

Emily watched as recognition sparked to life in Lady Griselda's eyes and she opened her mouth to address Emily, but Emily quelled her with a look and a small, frantic shake of her head. Biting her lip, she nodded almost imperceptibly toward Lord Winter.

Lady Griselda's eyes widened, and she flicked a glance up at the Viscount. "Who is this lovely creature?" she trilled. "Why have we not seen her before now? Where have you been hiding her? Sir Basil, have you ever seen such a lovely creature as this? Of course you haven't," she said, without waiting for him to respond. "Because there *is* no one like her, and you have never seen her before." She coughed delicately.

An expression of surprise flooded her husband's face, but he closed his mouth and said nothing.

Lord Winter made the necessary introduction — using her false surname, "Jones," which made Emily hold her breath, but neither of the older people goggled at it, bless them. Emily wilted in relief.

"Come," Lord Winter said. "Tea is waiting."

"Oh, I could not possibly—" Emily began, but Lady Griselda interrupted her.

"But of course you can, my dear! We insist."

"Oh!" Emily's eyes widened. Was that a veiled threat? She didn't think so, but she wasn't sure.

She curtsied. "Thank you, my lady. As you

wish." She wondered what would happen if the Hellions did make mischief while she was gone and implored God to remind them of their mother's gowns. Tea might take a while.

She needn't have worried, however.

Here in the country, tea was a shorter meal than in Town, and the guests were eager to leave it in favor of a planned afternoon of gossip, cards, strolling the grounds, and more gossip. It was over within an hour.

As she'd known by stealing a look at the guest list that morning, Sir Basil and Lady Griselda were the only ones present who knew her, and during tea Emily was able to relax, knowing they would not betray her. She'd always found the pair pleasant, but now she knew they were much more canny than they appeared and that they were kind, as well, for they didn't give the first hint that they were aware of her true identity.

In truth, she enjoyed herself, once she'd been introduced, deriving special pleasure from the disapproving glare of the harridan seated directly across from her. It was obvious the woman—Mrs. Kell-*something* was her name—did not approve of the governess's presence at tea. She looked as though she were tasting sour pickles every time their eyes met.

Emily was hard-pressed not to laugh out loud several times, for if the harridan knew who Emily really was, she would no doubt be groveling and fawning and declaring Emily an Original or some such claptrap.

In Town, Emily was a bit of a mystery. The only child of the Wealthy Winthrops of Windlay Square was an elusive prize, seldom seen but often spoken of. As the years passed with her still unwed, her fame grew. She was a bit of a heroine to the other spinsters of the *ton* and a trophy to be won amongst the unmarried gentlemen.

Emily looked around the large summer parlor where tea was held. Sooner or later, she supposed, the harridan *would* find out who Emily really was. Emily wished she could be there when it happened. How she would laugh!

She sipped her tea and pretended to listen to the lady sitting to her right, who was opining about the Prince and Brighton and Bath and Beau Brummel —none of whom she'd actually ever seen before with her own eyes. Emily had, unfortunately, and she found them all exceedingly dull. But she couldn't say so, of course, so she kept quiet.

This was the first time Emily had ever taken tea with the country set, and, apart from the harridan, she found the experience unexpectedly pleasant in spite of the necessity of maintaining her secrets.

The guest list included Dr. Brown, the village physician; several old landed squires, who between them apparently owned a considerable amount of property; and a few younger merchants and farmers, obviously prosperous, judging by the cut of their clothing. Most of the men—all but the doctor —were accompanied by their wives, and a few marriageable daughters and sons rounded out the company. It was a lively group.

Dr. Brown sat on her left, and Miss Emily Winthrop might have had a more satisfying conversation with him, but Emily *Jones* could not speak of her past experiences and could only converse in general terms. Dr. Brown didn't seem to notice and had stories enough to fill in, so Emily was free to keep watch on the Viscount, who looked handsome but rather stiff and uncomfortable presiding at the largest of the tea tables. She wondered if his demeanor would relax once he and his guests left the rather formal tea—not that she'd be there to see it, for she had to return to the nursery forthwith, of course.

At last tea was over, and as she made her way toward the parlor door, Lady Griselda touched her wrist. "A moment with you, my dear."

"Of course," Emily said, throwing a look toward Lord Winter, who was now speaking with the doctor.

They moved to one side of the room, and Lady Griselda whispered, "Tell me, my dear. Quickly, quickly!"

Emily hesitated. "I am here for a very good reason."

Lady Griselda smiled. "Of course you are, my dear. Avoiding the Duke of Besshire is the best of reasons."

"You know?"

"Doesn't everyone?" She winked. "Not to worry. I will not betray you, and neither will Sir Basil. Our lips are sealed."

"Thank you!" Emily whispered.

"Oh, no. Thank *you*, my dear. For you have turned a vastly dull house party into a much more intriguing one. Lord Winter is not what we were expecting—or hoping for, I am afraid."

"How so?"

"We thought he might be more ... well, more lively." She threw a warning look over Emily's shoulder. "Speak of the devil," she muttered and glided gracefully away.

Emily had to admit Lady Griselda was right. At tea, the Viscount had been completely respectable, which meant that he had also been completely boring. Stiff, inane, and formal. She saw nothing of the rambunctious boy that by all accounts he used to be.

And yet she refused to believe he had become like his parents, as some said. He was reviving some of the Christmas traditions they eschewed, after all, and his apology to Emily for his earlier set-down had been amiable and sincere.

What he needed was someone to reintroduce him to spontaneity, and Emily was the person to help with that, for if she were not spontaneous, no one was!

"My Dear Ophelia," Lady Griselda wrote late that night. *"I believe there is a young lady who could use your particular talents ..."* She ran the tip of her quill over her lips, pondering what to say next.

"Writing to Mrs. Robertson, my dear?" her

husband asked, coming into their bedchamber from the dressing room.

"How did you know?"

Sir Basil laughed. "If you are not together in a corner with your heads together, my dear, you are apart writing to each other. I never saw two ladies as thick as you are. One would think you were twins."

"We do think much alike."

"Indeed, heaven help me."

Lady Griselda *tsked* sympathetically. "Poor man. Perhaps you would like to sell your house on Grosvenor Square and move further away from her?" She threw him a mischievous, sidelong look, for he and Ophelia's husband John had become as attached to one another as she and Ophelia were. The four of them had a jolly time together and were rarely apart. The last thing on Earth her husband wanted was to end their association with the Robertsons.

"Minx," he said affectionately and looked over her shoulder. "Mind if I see what you are writing? Something about how handsome and virile your husband is, I wager." He bent to kiss her soundly.

Griselda returned his affectionate attention and

then batted him away with her quill. "Get on with you! I must ask Ophelia's advice."

"This would not be about Miss Emily Winthrop, would it?"

Griselda dimpled. "How did you guess? Ophelia is the most skilled matchmaker I ever knew. If she cannot bring them together, I do not know who can."

"Bring *whom* together?"

"Miss Winthrop and the Viscount Winter, of course."

Her husband gave a snort of surprise. "The Viscount? But he is—"

"A scapegrace? A rakehell? Not to worry," Griselda waved her quill. "He has reformed. Or at least he is trying."

Her husband's brow knitted below his wispy white hair. "So it seems. But that is not what worries me."

"What is it, then?"

"I worry he may succeed!" Basil sat down in a plump chair by the fire. "Did you see him at tea? Never saw a duller host."

"Miss Winthrop does not think him so."

"Bah! She was paying him no heed. Speaking with Dr. Brown the entire time. Rapt, she was."

"Men!" Griselda huffed. "You are all blind. Sir Basil, the good doctor *was* interested in Miss Winthrop, to be sure, but Miss Winthrop's attention was heavily divided—by the Viscount."

"But my love, Winter is busy building his reputation while Miss Jones is busy shredding hers."

"Indeed."

"How can you think the two of them are destined for each other?" he asked. But his wife only smiled enigmatically, and Sir Basil shrugged off his dressing gown and slid into bed, patting the empty space beside him. "If it is advice on the subject of love you need 'ere you embark on the matchmaker path yourself, perhaps I can offer my own assistance. A little research, perhaps?"

Griselda put down her quill and lay down beside him on the enormous four-poster. "Men!" she repeated with a shy smile. "I shall finish my letter later."

7

LIES AND REVELATIONS

IT SNOWED. THE ground was covered in white, and the guests' moods had become quite festive over the past two days. David congratulated himself on his timing. Christmas was the season of goodwill. He'd hang some greenery, light a fire, stuff everyone full of sweets, and everything would proceed just as he'd planned it.

It was late in the afternoon, and he was crossing the lawn on his way back from the ruins, where he'd been strolling with some of the younger set, when he came upon a battlefield: Miss Jones and the Hellions were having a snowball fight.

At first, he frowned. They should have been in the schoolroom, not cavorting outside. But they hadn't seen him yet, and as he stood for a moment, watching, he realized Rose and Rain were laughing so hard that they couldn't even toss their snowballs. And Miss Jones wasn't in much better shape.

He smiled in spite of himself. He'd never seen his children laughing like that. They were usually solemn around adults, but Miss Jones was an adult, and she was laughing right along with them!

He wished he could do that. *Should I be?* Guilt and regret stabbed him, but, just as quickly, he beat the emotions down. No, such behavior as Miss Jones was displaying wasn't what his children needed from him. He needed to maintain high expectations of them to ensure they grew up to be responsible. He would not be as rigid as his parents had been. He would be different. He would have a Yule log next year, too. But he wouldn't let his daughters remain Wild and Willful.

Still, it was difficult not to wave his arms and shout, "Look at me!" to provoke them. To join in the fun. Unconsciously, he raised his hand and took a step closer to them before stilling.

He'd almost done it, by Jove!

But he'd stopped himself, just in time. He had to be an example for his children. He had to behave respectably. Responsibly. And responsible adults did not become involved in snowball fights.

He turned to go, berating himself for the feeling of sadness that had suddenly come over him. It was not logical. It was not reasonable. It was not —

Thwack!

A snowball hit him right on his bottom!

David spun around. Behind him, Rose and Rain stood, uncertain, while Miss Jones stood grinning, her hand — the one that had previously held the enormous snowball — empty, her eyes sparkling with challenge.

He didn't think about what happened next. One moment he was fifty yards away from them, and the next, he was running, while simultaneously shaping an armload of scooped-up snow into the patriarch of all snowballs.

Three sets of eyes widened, three smiles appeared. And three girlish screams mixed with laughter erupted across the expanse of white.

They ran and David pursued, letting out a war whoop, an echo from his childhood. Freedom and pleasure and exhilaration rushed through him like a torrent, upwelling from his past, and David laughed.

He chased them until they ducked behind a snow wall, where they began lobbing bombs of cold and wet from the cache they'd hidden there. Taking cover behind a tree, he laughed some more. The war was on.

None of the snowballs hit their targets, but everyone enjoyed the battle. And when the ladies finally ran out of ammunition, they shrieked and ran, giggling and shouting. David grinned and chased after them, stopping long enough to load his arms with three huge snowballs, intending one for each of them. They had a good lead on him, but he was a fast runner. He overtook them just as he was rounding the corner of the icehouse and blindly threw the first snowball.

Which splattered—*thwack!*—right in the center of Mrs. Kellerman's forehead, before sliding down over her face and chins and falling with a *plop* into her enormous *décolletage!*

David froze.

"What is the meaning of this?" she thundered, wiping snow from her eyes. "Outrageous! Who threw that?"

David dropped the two snowballs he held and reflexively smoothed back his errant lock of hair.

"Lord Winter!" she blustered. "Did you throw that missile?"

Miss Jones and the Hellions were nowhere to be

seen. "I apologize, Mrs. Kellerman. I was playing with my children," he said.

"That I do not doubt!" she said. "You always excelled at play, young man. I trust other aspects of your personality have not remained the same." She turned away, dismissing him haughtily.

David closed his eyes and, smoothing his hair yet again, sighed heavily and groaned. She was the biggest stickler in the neighborhood. The person least likely to rush to give him a loan. Matriarch of the richest family in Buxley-on-Isis. An arbiter of personal decorum. The one person he needed to impress the very most. And he'd just plastered her with a snowball.

Emily came skulking from around the far corner of the icehouse just in time to see the harridan walking stiffly away from Lord Winter. Neither looked happy.

Uh-oh …

Before Emily could stop them, Rose and Rain rushed from behind her and ran at their father brandishing fresh snowballs. Holding up his palm, he quelled their enthusiasm with a baleful look. The joy in their little faces evaporated, and Emily glared. It was easy to see that they were hurt.

Emily gestured toward the small cluster of trees that ran along the edge of the wide lawn. "Run along, ladies, and gather ivy and holly for the kissing boughs," she said quietly.

"Are you going to argue with Papa again?" Rain asked.

"Nonsense. We are having a lovely time, are we not? There is nothing at all to argue about."

That seemed to satisfy them both, and they scampered away on an eager search for greenery.

"What is wrong?" she asked Lord Winter as soon as the girls were out of earshot.

He scowled. "What is wrong is that you have turned the place upside down!"

She felt as though he had struck her, and her face must have reflected it, for he was instantly contrite.

"No, no! I am sorry. I did not mean that." He looked down at the ground and shook his head. "What happened is entirely my fault. I should not have lost control as I did."

"Lost control!" she cried, incredulous. "What do you mean 'lost control?' I'd say you embraced spontaneity."

"Exactly."

She shook her head. "And what, may I ask, is wrong with that?"

"Rash behavior leads inevitably to doom, Miss Jones."

She planted her hands on her hips. "What *doom* can possibly have befallen you because you were tossing a few little snowballs?"

"One of those 'little snowballs' hit Mrs. Kellerman."

Emily couldn't have kept her bark of laughter down if she'd tried—which she didn't.

"How dare you laugh!"

"Forgive me, my lord!" she said, chortling the while, "but I do find it funny, for Mrs. Kellerman is exactly the type of woman I wish to avoid. London was full of them, haughty, self-righteous, disdainful Town pugs, snapping and quarreling amongst themselves."

Quarreling over me. She sobered and gave an involuntary shudder.

He rolled his eyes skyward. "Though I will concede that Mrs. Kellerman is not a great favorite of mine, she is still my guest—and as such you will treat her with respect, whether she is present or not."

"Of course, my lord," Emily said, knowing he was right. "I am too outspoken. It is one of my faults." She would have thought Lord Winter would be satisfied with her capitulation, but, inexplicably, he scowled.

"You hail from London?" he asked. "I thought you said you came from the North."

Emily's heart gave a flutter. "Oh, I ... I did, but ... that is to say, I ... I am not originally from the North, my lord, but from London." Which was true enough. Emily was born in Grosvenor Square at the very height of the London Season, and she'd been an inconvenience to her parents ever since—one they fervently wished to be rid of.

"I see," said the Viscount, and Emily felt a stab of guilt, for she knew he did not see clearly at all. No, she was obscuring his view at every turn, and it chafed at her. Secrecy was not in her nature. In fact, she was often accused of being too forthright. It was one of "the Emily crosses" her mother bore—vocally and with much relish.

As though reading her thoughts, he said, "Come to think of it, I know precious little about you, Miss Jones. If I am to write a letter of reference, there are certain questions I should ask you."

It was by sheer force of will that Emily held

herself still and swallowed down the lump that formed instantly in her throat. "Go on," she said evenly, though her heart was trying to pound its way out of her chest.

For the next five minutes, Lord Winter asked her personal questions. She answered truthfully whenever she could, but most of what she said were half-truths and lies of omission. And when the Viscount was finished asking questions and had disappeared into the house, Emily was left behind with a deep sense of shame and guilt.

He'd been kind enough to take her in and give her employment—when she was alone and starving, for all he knew. And here she was, lying to him, spoiling his children, and keeping an elephant hidden away in his barn without his permission.

She thought about him all the rest of that afternoon and evening. His frown, his scowl, his glare ... his smile, his laugh, his shining eyes, his ridiculous war whoop.

More than once, her mind went a-begging, reliving the moment when her snowball had hit his well-shaped rump and he'd turned around and let fly that outrageous battle cry and then thrown his head back and laughed with complete, glorious abandon.

She wondered if he was even aware that he'd laughed at all.

It was late. David had been working in his study ever since his last guest went to bed. Thank goodness they did not keep Town hours! He set his spectacles down and rubbed the bridge of his nose. He couldn't concentrate. He kept thinking about having lost his temper with Miss Jones. Why had he been such an ass?

He'd scared himself, that was why. He'd scared himself with that savage cry he'd given and that willy-nilly snowball fight and the utter lack of restraint he'd shown.

He couldn't afford to go back to the way he'd been before the war.

But, blast if he hadn't enjoyed himself!

David couldn't remember the last time he'd laughed like that. And his children had laughed right along with him. His children and Miss Jones ...

He drifted into a memory of the snowball fight. How lovely his little girls had looked, their eyes sparkling with excitement ... how lovely *she'd* looked, with her cheeks all pink and her dress flipped up over her ankles and her expression full of joyful defiance! She was so unlike any other lady he knew.

"I … saw the light …"

As though he'd conjured her with the memory, there she was, her slender form silhouetted in the doorway of his study. She was holding a tray with a pot and two cups on it. He could see steam rising.

She nodded toward the single lamp on his desk. "I can see the light through my window in the nursery wing. You work in here at night by the light of that one lamp," she said. "And, with the snow today and no fire on the hearth … well, I thought you might be cold."

For a few seconds, he didn't know what to say. He wasn't used to anyone making a fuss over his comfort. Finally, he settled on a simple, "Thank you."

She set the tray down on his desk. "A peace offering of sorts. I do not know how to make coffee, but I do know how to make chocolate. Have you ever had it? I make it for myself in the middle of the night, sometimes," she confessed. "When it's available," she added. "Cook had a bit extra. I hope you do not mind my using it."

"Not at all."

She poured them both a cup of the thick, brown brew, and David tasted it. It was hot and bitter and surprisingly good. He thought about remarking about it being a "peace offering," but he didn't want to spoil the moment. It was good to sit there in companionable silence with her. *With anyone*, he corrected himself. He remembered his wife visiting his study. Rebecca had been shy and timid, and he hadn't really been able to talk with her, so they'd also sat in silent companionship. But it hadn't been the same as sitting with Miss Jones.

Miss Jones, who was most definitely not shy and timid!

"Why do you have to conserve so, my lord?" she asked suddenly. "No fire on your hearth, only one lamp, and so little food."

"Why do you have to pry?" he countered, not truly offended. After all, she had warned him she was direct.

"Because that is the sort of person I am," she answered. "I ask because I have questions."

"Do you always do things without regard for the consequences?"

"'Leap and the net will appear,'" she quoted him with a grin.

"I also said, 'Leap often enough, and someday the net will *not* appear.' What would you have done if I'd taken offense at your impertinent question and dismissed you just now? Where would you have gone? Where would you have slept?"

"I do not know." She shrugged. "But things would have settled themselves favorably, I am sure. They always do."

"That sort of attitude leads inevitably to disaster." He tapped the newspaper on a side table. "The papers are always full of such stories."

"You exaggerate," she said, scooping up the paper and opening it up.

To prove him wrong, he supposed. She obviously intended to read the wedding announcements or some dry financial information or an advertisement for a hair tonic. But, her eyes scanned the paper for only a moment before they widened and she snapped the newspaper shut.

He choked down a laugh. "Oh, yes. Pray do read it. I haven't the time for it."

For the second time that day, Emily felt her heart trying to beat its way out of her chest. She'd seen her name in the paper. Her *real* name. "Ah ... since you do not read the paper, may I have it, please? Thank you!" she said, not waiting for a reply and, tucking the paper under her arm, she stood up—too quickly, for she accidentally swiped the paper across the corner of his desk and knocked to the floor several small objects there. "Oh! I am so sorry!" she cried and bent to pick them up.

"No, no! Leave them. They are of no importance," he said, looking vaguely uncomfortable.

"Nonsense," she said, replacing the things on his desk.

They were tiny silver figures. A hedgehog, a frog, a horse, a lamb, a bell, a sixpence, a pea, and a bean. Suddenly, Emily realized what they were and laughed with delight. "These are favors for mixing into a plum pudding!"

He nodded. "Cook asked me to keep them in my study until Twelfth Night. It is one place the Hellions never go," he explained. "She wants them to be surprised."

He looked embarrassed, and she wondered why. But for once, she did not pry. "Of course," she said quietly, and they drank the rest of the chocolate in silence before Emily beat a hasty retreat, taking the tray and her incriminating newspaper with her.

After a stop in the kitchen to drop off the tray, she headed for the stairs. But her path took her right past the study once more, and she followed an impulse to peek in on the puzzling Viscount.

Creeping to the door and peering past it, her eyes goggled, for there was he was—the rigid, responsible Viscount Winter—*playing* with the Twelfth Night favors, a gentle, little-boy smile on his face, and, instantly, Emily Winthrop, the improbable, imposter governess, realized she was in love.

8

FOOLISH THOUGHTS

*E*MILY LAY AWAKE for a long time, slept fitfully for a few hours, and finally gave up a little after dawn. Padding down to the darkened kitchens, she broke her fast with a slice of thick, sweet milk bread with butter and a cup of cold milk.

Cook and her assistant bustled here and there, preparing breakfast and singing. Presently, Gertie came in.

"Bless me," Gertie exclaimed, catching sight of Emily, "What are you doing down here so early, miss? Wild and Willful awake already?"

"No, they're still asleep, and I expect they will be for another hour or two at least."

"Why is that?"

"Rain had a nightmare that awakened all of us,

so we had a little midnight picnic of warm milk and a story. It took me forever to get them back to sleep, and then I could not get back to sleep myself."

"Mmm," the girl intoned. "You look it, if you don't mind me saying. Tired eyes. But who wouldn't be tired after being chained to Wild and Willful for three days?" Gertie patted her hand. "I daresay you need a holiday." She *tsked* as she filled a cup from the coffee pot Cook had prepared and sat at the wide, kitchen table. "Tell you what," she said, pulling a slip of paper from her apron. "Cook was going to send me into Buxley Village to buy a few things she needs, but I don't have much else to do this morning, not until the guests start wakin' up, anyway. How about you go instead of me? Take yourself a little walk. 'Tis a fine morning, if a little cold, and I expect a little alone time would do you good."

Emily beat down a giggle. She'd never been urged to walk alone. In fact, she'd been forbidden. It wasn't proper for young ladies to walk unchaperoned—unless they were governesses or serving maids or tavern girls or milkmaids and such. Of course, she'd been walking alone for most of this past month, but that was different; being alone this past month had been an act of rebellion. Gertie thought nothing of Emily walking about unaccompanied. It was normal.

Emily dimpled, and Gertie took that as agreement. "Good then. I'll take myself on up to the nursery and watch the little 'uns until you get back."

"Oh, but I could not ask you to —"

"Oh, ho-ho! Yes you can!" Cook said. "I see what our *generous* Miss Gertie is all about. She's hoping to snabble herself a little nap while you're gone."

In confirmation, Gertie waggled her eyebrows and grinned. "I'll sleep on the cot near the children, miss, and tie strings to their nightrails so I'll wake up if they do." She laughed. "A little trick Miss Bull uses, I hear."

"Oh!"

"It's barely half-past-seven now," Gertie urged, "and I won't be needed around here for another three hours, long enough for quite the ramble for you."

Emily lifted her chin to peer out the kitchen window. "But the ground is covered in snow."

"Oh," Gertie said dejectedly, then brightened. "I know! You can make for the Drum and Goat. That's the coaching inn down there in Buxley Village. It's small, but there's a nice, cosy little common room.

You can warm up there before you start back. The ostler's wife makes the best tea this side of Mayfair, and for breakfast she serves it with the loveliest berry scones. All for just two farthings!"

Emily lowered her eyes. "I am afraid I have not been paid yet."

Reaching into her apron pocket, Gertie took out a penny and slid it over to Emily. "A loan until you're paid."

"Oh! I ... I couldn't take your—"

"Take it, the girl wants a nap, and she'll be much less sour around here after she gets it!" Cook grinned over her shoulder, earning an answering smile from Gertie.

Emily pasted on a mock-serious expression and took the coin. "I believe a ramble down the lane *would* do me some good. Thank you, Gertie."

Taking an apple from the cupboard, Emily motioned to Gertie, and they climbed the stairs to the nursery where Gertie insisted upon setting up the cot right next to Rose and Rain's beds. As Emily quit the room, she was tying a length of twine to the ribbon on Rose's nightrail, as she'd promised she would.

Emily headed for the stables, where she intended to deliver her apple to Baby, but when she arrived, the little elephant was asleep, curled in the hay and tucked in underneath two woolen horse blankets. Emily smiled and slid the apple into her cloak pocket. She would deliver the treat later.

It was much too snowy to ramble over the pastures or through the woods, but the lane was flat, dry, and walkable, so she strode briskly down the lane and then the main road. Buxley Village was only two and a half miles away, but it was even colder than she'd thought, and she was chilled to the bone by the time she arrived at the Drum and Goat.

She was greeted as she came in through the door with "Well, if it isn't Miss Jones! I wondered when we would see you here." Emily peered into the dimly lit interior to find the plump figure of a woman bustling behind the bar of the common room. "I'm Mrs. Dumfries, the ostler's wife. Coffee or tea?" she asked.

"Tea, please, ma'am," answered a surprised Emily. "How did you know who I am?"

The woman laughed as though Emily had told the finest joke she'd ever heard. "Well, bless me, who else would you be?" She laughed some more as she moved off toward the kitchen. "I'll be back in two shakes of a lamb's tail!"

Emily looked around. The room was crowded

with ancient, scarred, oaken tables. At one end, a couple of narrow logs burned weakly in a small, stone fireplace. A single lamp burned at the end of the bar. As she peered into the gloom, she saw a figure at one of the tables near the back corner. His head rested upon folded arms, and he was emitting soft, regular breathing noises. She tilted her head. He was impeccably dressed and possessed curly, dark hair …

"Lord Winter?"

David awakened with a start.

"Lord Winter?" the voice repeated. "My lord?"

He lifted his head and, squinting, rubbed his neck as a woman approached. "Yes? Who is it?"

"Your governess," she said, stepping up to the table and pulling out a chair. "Or your children's governess, rather—though by the look of you, perhaps you could use one, too." She sat down. "You look terrible."

"You too."

She chuckled. "I could not sleep."

"Me either."

"Well, not at home in your bed, I see. How long

have you been here?"

"What time is it?" David turned to peer at the window, where he saw that the rising sun had painted the eastern sky a rosy pink.

"About a quarter after eight."

He watched her take off her bonnet, heavy cloak, and woolen scarf. "I have only been here for an hour or so," he said. "I came for the tea." He motioned toward the half-empty cup of cold tea that sat on the table beside him. "Mrs. Dumfries is famous for her tea."

"So I hear." She sat down without being asked.

"Please. Sit," David invited with a raised eyebrow. She threw him a cheeky grin, and David couldn't help being charmed. "The Hellions still asleep, I presume?"

She nodded. "Gertie is watching them. It was Gertie who insisted I walk into the village. She said I looked terrible."

"You do," David agreed again, thinking just the opposite. In truth, she was actually quite adorable, with her high cheekbones and small nose pinkened from the cold.

He stilled. How long had she been out in the cold? Bending to the side, he glanced down at her snow-covered boots.

"Did you *walk* here?" he asked.

She chuckled. "A governess can hardly order up the carriage, my lord. It isn't her place."

She was correct. It *wasn't* her place. But it didn't feel right. He watched as she pulled off her gloves and laid them aside and imagined what her hands would look like encased in fine, white kid instead of coarse, brown wool. She would have cut a fine dash though the ballrooms of London, had life treated her as it should have.

Mrs. Dumfries arrived with an enormous steaming pot of tea and a plate of fresh, warm scones.

Miss Jones straightened. "Mmm. I am suddenly famished."

"Did you not break your fast before you left Stendmore Park?"

"I did."

"What did you have?" David asked, not quite knowing why he should take an interest in a governess's breakfast habits.

"A slice of bread with butter and a cup of cold milk."

"That is all?" David was shocked. "You should have asked Cook to provide something more filling."

"I did not want it, my lord. "At home, I always

eat … a*te*," she corrected herself. "I always ate bread and butter for breakfast." She pulled a scone from the plate and began to eat, keeping her eyes averted, and David got the impression that she was using the pastry as a shield to deflect further questions. He decided to let her be.

Picking up a cup and saucer, she tasted the tea. "Oh, la, this *is* delicious tea! Gertie said Mrs. Dumfries's tea was amazingly good, and now I see why. What is in this? How does she do it?"

"No one knows. She will not divulge her recipe."

"Well then, I shall just have to keep—" She stopped mid-sentence and busied herself with her napkin. It was obvious she would have finished with "keep coming here," or some such.

David reached over and brushed his fingers over hers. "It will turn out right in the end. You will see. We shall find you another position. A good position."

She forced a smile. "One where the village ostler's wife makes the most delicious tea in England?"

He nodded. "Most assuredly."

"Well then. I am saved." *She* patted *his* hand this time, and David's skin tingled. He frowned. Tingly skin was bad. A miserable sign. A portent of danger.

She's trouble, old man, and you should stay far, far away from her, he told himself. *In fact, you should stand up and leave. Right now.*

But he didn't. Instead, he found himself inexplicably delaying their parting, picking at his own scone and sipping his tea and watching, fascinated, as she ate. She had the manners of a lady. Delicate, fastidious, graceful. Her hands were white and small and smooth, and David couldn't help wondering what they'd feel like clasped in his, if they walked back home together.

Stop it. He hadn't walked this morning, he'd ridden Thor. And he was most assuredly not offering to allow her to ride with him. The last thing David needed was for Miss Jones to nestle against his—

He looked away.

"Something wrong?" she asked.

"No. Ah … are you planning to do some shopping?" He nodded toward the thick, green woolen bag she carried. Someone, long ago, judging by the broken, faded threads, had embroidered the front of the bag with *"Stendmore Park."*

She nodded. "A few things for Cook. I have a list. Though I do not know where to find the shops."

Accompanying her while she shopped could do

no harm. "Well." He pasted on a serious expression. "Buxley-on-Isis *is* very large and confusing."

"It is?"

"Oh, yes. Quite so. And a young lady wandering alone could become lost."

"This is it?" Emily asked, a few minutes later. "Buxley-on-Isis has but a single high street and some houses. Why, I can see three *barns* from here! It would be impossible for me to become lost."

"You are right. Buxley is quite small."

"Then why did you say otherwise?"

"Because I wanted to accompany you. Is that so impossible to believe? There is the chandler's shop."

She said nothing until he reached for the knob on the door of the little shop. Then she put out her hand and touched his sleeve. "I am a servant, my lord," she said quietly. "Were you a craftsman or a shopkeeper or a farmer, you could escort me inside. It would go unremarked. But as it is, people will think—" Her eyes met his for a one second ...two ... and then she took her hand away. "I can manage on my own. I am sure your guests could use your help more than I."

She was right. The truth hit David between the eyes: everything had changed the day Robert died. David was no longer the younger son. A commoner. He was a viscount, and she was a servant. Before she became impoverished, before he became a Peer of the Realm, they could have wed without anyone thinking it unusual. But now their difference in status was an insurmountable wall. The villagers would ask themselves why a Viscount was squiring his children's governess about. And they would talk. Even servants had reputations to uphold.

He didn't know what to say, so in the end he said nothing at all. After executing a crisp bow, he turned and strode briskly back the way they'd come.

Emily watched him go, and for the first time, the enormity of her situation struck her. She wasn't a servant. Or was she?

Time spread out before her like a river delta, a forking tree of possible futures.

How she would relish her parents' expressions when she returned to London and told them what she'd done! She would threaten to spread the tale of her adventures herself if they did not relent and allow her to return to her father's country estate and be left in peace. They would be furious. Mortified. And defeated. It would be glorious!

Or …

They could keep her in London forever. Forever pursued and hounded by an endless stream of hopeful, gold-digging suitors, who would only become more odious each year as she grew further into spinsterhood and lost her bloom. And someday Lord Winter would find out who she was.

Her mouth drew into a grim line.

How would the Viscount react to the truth? What would he say to her when they met once again in London, as they inevitably would?

"Excuse me, miss," a small voice said at her elbow. "I need to get in there." The little boy gestured at the door Emily was blocking. "My mum will have my hide if I don't get back home with the candles right quick-like."

"Of course," Emily murmured, moving aside.

Tiny snowflakes were dancing on the hint of a breeze as she stepped into the chandler's shop. Six thick, beeswax candles went into her bag and then it was on to the spice-shop and the grocer.

By the time her errands for Cook were finished, the snow was falling in earnest and swirling in a rising breeze. Emily shivered and hurried down the street toward Stendmore Park. The temperature was dropping, and even in her woolen gloves, her hands were cold. Her toes were starting to hurt. Briefly, she thought of stopping once more at The Drum and Goat to warm herself but thought better of it. If the storm grew any worse, it might not be safe to make the trip home.

Home. Wouldn't it be lovely if Stendmore Park really were her home?

Emily shrugged off the foolish thought. Stendmore Park wasn't her home, any more than any of her parents' grand estates were. Emily didn't have a home, not really. The places she'd lived all belonged to her father, and it had been clear since the day she'd turned seven and her father had declared he had only to put up with her for one more decade that she wasn't welcome at any of them.

As she passed by one of the village's outlying farms, she heard muted laughter and lively music from a concertina. Light shone invitingly from inside the farmer's cottage, and inside she saw two figures dancing. How Emily wished she could ask to come inside! It looked like they were having fun. It looked like they belonged.

All at once she felt more alone than she'd ever felt.

The edges of the lane were lost in fresh snow, now. She kept her head down and her eyes on the ground. Only a two miles or so to go.

"There you are!"

Emily recognized the voice immediately and looked up: the Viscount. He was sitting atop his large, black gelding, wearing a greatcoat, tall hat, scarf, and gloves. The rim of his hat bore an inch of snow. He'd obviously been waiting there for her for some time.

Wordlessly, he put out his hand, and Emily looked down at her shopping bag. "That is very kind of you, my lord, but I can manage. It is not very heavy," she lied.

He threw her a look, shook his head, and kept his arm extended, palm up.

"Oh, very well," Emily said, handing him the bag, which he tied to his saddle. Then, he stuck his arm out again and raised his eyebrow.

Emily shook her head. "I can walk," she said.

"Miss Jones, I know it is not proper for a young lady to ride on the back of a horse with a gentleman. But it is not proper for a young lady to be walking alone in the first place, is it?" He didn't wait for her to answer. "And there is no one here to witness the impropriety of your riding with me. I will let you down as we approach Stendmore Park, and you can walk the rest of the way with none the wiser. I cannot in good conscience, allow a lady to walk two miles in the snow. I would hate to see your toes frostbitten." As if to punctuate his words, the sound of distant thunder rolled over them. "Thunder snow," he said, looking at the sky ominously. "We had best get moving. Up you come!"

He had brought his horse to a stop next to a stump. *Leap and the net shall appear*, she thought as she stepped up, took his outstretched hand, and placed her foot in the stirrup that his foot had vacated so that she could mount. There were worse things than riding through the snow on the back of a horse with a handsome gent—

"Oh, la!" Emily exclaimed as she was suddenly lifted to a spot not behind the saddle, but in front of the Viscount.

"Easy," he said, and Emily wasn't sure if he were talking to the gelding or to her. "Settle down, now." He urged the horse to a walk.

Without benefit of sidesaddle and with her skirts wrapped around her legs, Emily was rather unsteady, though she needn't have worried. She was in no danger of slipping off with the Viscount's left arm wrapped securely around her waist.

"How is that?" he asked. "Comfortable?"

"Yes. Very," she lied.

"Lovely day, is it not?" he asked a minute later, as though they were not experiencing anything more remarkable than a walk along Pall Mall.

"Lovely," she agreed, trying to keep her balance.

They rode on for a minute before he said, "Miss Jones, you would be more comfortable—and I less worried for your safety—if you leaned against me."

"Oh. I am sorry." She said and attempted to do as he asked, but it was difficult, when her skin tingled wherever they touched and her—

"What the blazes is *that*?" he asked suddenly. "Thor, halt!"

The well-trained horse stopped instantly, and Emily sat up again. "What is what?"

"This," said the Viscount, his hand questing between them at the juncture of his thighs. "There is something large and uncomfortable here."

Something large and uncomfortable? There? "My lord!" Emily screeched and slid from the horse. Falling to the ground, she stumbled and rolled onto her back in the snow.

"Miss Jones!" the Viscount cried. "Are you

hurt?" He jumped down and knelt beside her, dropping the reins. The gelding danced nervously away, but quickly stilled. She had more good training to thank for that, Emily supposed. "Too bad you and your horse do not have more in common, my lord!" she cried. "Good training and a good gelding!"

"Beg pardon?" The Viscount reeled as though he had been slapped.

It was only then that Emily noticed the apple he held in his hand—the forgotten apple she'd been carrying in her cloak pocket all day. The *large* and *uncomfortable* apple. A nervous giggle bubbled up from somewhere deep inside and blossomed into a full, throaty chuckle.

"I take it you are all right," he said drily.

She nodded and continued to laugh, and the more perplexed he looked, the funnier she found the situation. "I—I am … I am s—sorry," she finally managed. "I—I did not mean to accuse you. That is, I—I *did* mean it, but …" Her words faded into gales of nervous laughter. She could no more have stopped herself from laughing than she could have stopped the snow from falling.

The Viscount, clearly attempting to make sense of her odd behavior, was staring at the apple in his hand, his lips moving silently as his mind replayed the last few seconds. And then, sudden clarity appeared in the form of shock, and then mortification. His gaze snapped back to Emily, and he too began to laugh.

It was a curious moment. Emily had never behaved so wantonly, so brazenly. Her behavior was beyond the pale. And the Viscount knew that. Yet he wasn't shocked. He didn't show any sign of disapproval. Instead, he joined in and laughed with her.

It was good to be a servant!

When their sides were no longer heaving and they could speak, he cleared his throat dramatically and offered Emily his hand. "Shall we continue?" he said with a lopsided smile.

"Indeed," Emily said and bent to pick up her reticule, which had slipped from her wrist and lay on the ground.

David handed her the apple and then, this time, lifted her onto the saddle and swung up behind her. Thor accepted the odd arrangement nicely, and David urged him back onto the lane. They said nothing for the next mile. She leaned against him without his having to ask, and David found himself wishing she wasn't wearing a hat. He would have liked to have nestled his chin against her soft hair.

At least he imagined it would be soft. He'd found himself imagining all sorts of things these past four days.

As they rode on, he tried not to think about how natural she felt nestled against his chest. About how much he wanted to allow his hand to curl across her belly and pull her against him harder, harder …

He felt his groin tighten and growled.

"Hmm?" she said.

He coughed as an alibi and said, "We are approaching the East gate of Stendmore Park. Just over that rise is the stable. I will drop you off just before the gate and cut back across the field so we are not seen alone together. I have to visit the Smith's place before I head home anyway."

"What smiths? Do you mean 'Smiths?' Or *black*smiths?"

"The former," he answered. "William Smith. One of the estate's tenant farmers. His wife gifted him with a new baby. A fine son born just yesterday, and I promised him I would come have a look today."

He felt her body tense, "Oh! May I—" She stilled and then sagged against him. "It was on the tip of my tongue to ask if I could tag along," she said in a dejected tone. "I love little babies."

He could feel her disappointment, and he wondered how many babies she'd held. In her former life, as a parson or landed squire's daughter, she'd probably made many such visits.

At that moment, a sound reached them, a curious, horn-like sort of—

Miss Jones began to cough violently.

The trumpeting happened again. "That sounds like an—an *elephant!*" David laughed.

"An *elephant!*" Miss Jones laughed out loud. "Oh, yes, my lord. I forgot to mention, I brought with me an elephant and have been secretly keeping it out in your stable."

David chuckled. "And you have a lion in the cellar, I suppose?"

"Indeed, and a giraffe in the nursery."

"I am unsurprised."

"And I am … I am *hungry!*" she said suddenly.

"Me too. Mrs. Dumfries's scones seem years away."

"Here," Emily said, holding up the apple. "Eat this."

"I would love to," he answered, but I am afraid
my hands are quite encumbered at the moment." He
was holding Thor's reins with one hand and her
with the other, so she did what any thoughtful,
reasonable young lady would have done. What any
mad, unapologetic, unchecked hoyden might have
done.

She raised the apple to his mouth and gently
pushed it against his lips, urging him to take a bite.

He did.

It was the best apple he had ever tasted.

Feeding him that apple was the most irresponsible,
most outrageous, most unforgettable thing Emily
had ever done. The thing was done in total silence.
No conversation spoiled the biting, crunching, and
swallowing, and every moment was electric. She
leaned against his warmth, the rhythm of the
walking horse rocking them into an even warmer
place, and Emily wished the apple would last
forever. Wished the ride would last forever.

They didn't, of course.

"Well," he said, pulling up before the yellow
stone gate that marked the beginning of the long

lane that lead to Stendmore Park. "Here we are." He dismounted and, curling his large, warm hands around Emily's waist, lifted her down as though she were but a bit of fluff.

He was strong and big and excruciatingly masculine, and for a moment, time stopped. Then, he dropped his hands and stood before her. Emily didn't look into his eyes. "Well," she echoed.

She thought he hesitated just a bit too long before asking, "Was there anything else?"

Was there? Silently, she shook her head and curtsied.

"Good day." He bowed and mounted his horse once more. As Emily watched him ride away, she felt a tension build inside her, an explosive force she couldn't ignore. "Lord Winter!" she called.

He stopped and turned in the saddle.

She took a step forward. "Was … was my being able to catch Rose and Rain the only reason you wanted my feet to remain intact, my lord?"

"By no means," he said, smiling. "I also wanted you to be able to dodge giant, man-sized snowballs, should any come flying at you from out of nowhere." He tipped his hat. "Good day, Miss Jones!"

9

THE KISSING BOUGH

THOUGH THE MOON was but a waning crescent, now, it seemed to dance off the snow and into Emily's eyes. She couldn't sleep.

Her head was still full of the moment she'd brought the apple to his lips, and he'd bitten down.

What did she want from him? Did she expect him to declare his love for his children's penniless governess? Did she expect him to ask her to marry him? Nonsense!

He was attracted to her, that was plain. But that wasn't enough.

Mud and dirt!

Her own parents were not—and had never been —in love. "Love is a convenience one can do without," her mother had said, over and over. "Money is what makes a good marriage, not 'the finer feelings.'" But little Emily Winthrop hadn't been able to see why one could not have both.

After listening to muted arguing from outside her parents' bedroom one evening when she was but eight years old, Emily had gone to her room and sworn to her candle-lit image in the looking glass that she would never marry without love.

The trouble was, she'd learned when she was old enough to court, it was impossible to tell if a man loved and desired her or if he simply loved and desired the mountain of money her parents were openly willing to settle upon her.

David Stendmore needed money, and he was certainly attracted to her, but he certainly did not love her. If she told him she was the only child and heir of the "Wealthy Winthrops" and he declared his love and asked her to marry him, would she accept?

How could she? But how could she not? She loved the deuced man!

She lay awake for another hour before rising and putting on her wrapper, a heavy cloak, and her walking boots. It was late, close on dawn. The girls were tucked into their beds, fast asleep, and the nursery fire was safely banked and glowing. After assuring herself that all was well, she slipped outside, thinking the cold night air might help to clear her head of the emotions that swirled there like snow, obscuring reason. But it was too cold, and her traitorous feet carried her to the warmth of the glasshouse where the moon's light bathed everything in a luminous blue-white.

"Dear God," she whispered. "How could I have let this happen?" How could she have fallen in love with someone so unsuitable? She didn't even like him. At least, she didn't like the man he was trying to become. And *he* certainly did not like *her*. She sighed heavily.

After their ride together, Emily hadn't even *seen* the Viscount the rest of the day. He had not met her and the girls while they were on their afternoon ramble about the grounds. He did not insist that Emily attend tea. He hadn't even come to the nursery to say goodnight to his girls.

And then, like a dream—or a nightmare, she wasn't sure which—he appeared in the doorway of the glasshouse.

"What are you doing here?" she demanded, her voice cracking. *Stupid question. Stupid, stupid.*

"I am working," he said.

"Of course you are," she said. "I should have

known. Do men not always work in the small hours of the morning in their glasshouses in the middle of winter?"

"I was working in my study," he said, "and my eyes started to cross. I needed to stretch my legs." He held up his hand, his fingers wrapped around a ball of twine. "I roll it off the roof outside and catch it. It helps me think. But I saw you inside, so here I am instead."

"I will wager you never come here during the day," she said.

"What do you mean?"

"Only that you pretend to be what you are not. You pretend to be all business, when in truth, you would like to play."

He scowled but issued no denials. "What are you doing here?"

"I could not sleep," she said.

"Is something troubling you?"

"Indeed, my lord, there is. But I do not wish to burden you with my bumblebroth."

"Nonsense," he said with a disarming smile. "If you did not wish to burden me with it you would not have mentioned it."

"You are right, of course," she said.

"Of course," he said, deliberately arrogant.

She laughed. "Be careful with those jests, my lord, or someone will learn your secrets."

"I have no secrets."

"No. Not at first glance. But you are more than you seem, and I find myself on uneven ground. Frankly, I do not know what to make of you. I wonder ..." She regarded him thoughtfully. "Since you interrogated me about myself earlier, I wonder if you will answer some questions about yourself?"

"You may feel free to ask whatever you like," he said, "and I shall feel free to answer your questions as truthfully as you did."

She looked at him sharply, and one masculine brow climbed high upon his forehead. "You are very astute," she said. "You know I was not completely honest with you when you questioned me about my past."

"Not completely honest?" he asked. "Miss Jones, I reckon very little of what you told me was unvarnished truth."

She could feel her cheeks stain themselves pink. "I am not accustomed to telling lies," she said.

"If I thought you were, I would have dismissed you and had one of my men escort you from my land."

She waited for him to demand she divulge her

secrets, but the moment stretched into seconds, and he stood mute, regarding her with an expression of ... of what? Respect? Is that what she saw there? Because she knew it was not admiration. No. He thought her impulsive and undisciplined, everything he despised.

"It is true that I am grateful for your kindness," she said.

He held up one hand. "Your secrets are your own. I believe all people of good character are entitled to them."

"You have decided I am good, then, my lord?"

"I have."

"And what led you to that conclusion?"

"Your reaction to Mrs. Kellerman at tea."

She gave an unladylike snort. "I was exceedingly vexed with her and all but ignored her—when I was not impatient and even strident. How can that have led you to the conclusion that I am good?"

"Some would call your behavior honesty."

"And others would call it impertinence, as you yourself pointed out to me. Did you in truth hit her with that snowball?"

"Right in the middle of her forehead. And the bulk of the snow slid into her gown." Unexpectedly, a chuckle escaped him. "I used to plot against her as a child—though the worst I ever did was steal apples from her orchard."

"Of course. For you are every bit as good a person as I am. Lord Winter's heart isn't quite as cold as he wishes everyone to believe."

"What do you mean by that?" he asked. "No!" He held up his palm. "I do not wish to know." He looked like he wanted to say something else, but then, suddenly, he bowed and moved toward the door.

"Lord Winter," she called after him. "I wonder if I might take the children into the village tomorrow to buy some watercolors and some paper. The children want to illustrate their stories."

"What?" He tilted his head. "Are you are still allowing them to indulge in fantasy?"

"I am afraid I am," she said, trying hard not to look contrite.

He frowned. "Miss Jones, I thought I told you that we must set limits, and they must learn to accept them!"

Emily was tired of all his talk of rules and limits. *Balderdash!* She knew it was claptrap, and it was time someone pointed it out to him. "Must they also be rebuffed by their father as they were yesterday?

To have their creativity strangled out of them? To be bored to tears?"

"What rubbish!"

"Rubbish? That is exactly what happened when you dismissed their stories two days ago and again yesterday when you dismissed *them*!"

"I did *not!*"

"You did!" She stamped her foot for emphasis. "They rushed at you with smiles and snowballs and you scowled and held up your palm—like this!" She parodied the motion with her own palm and frowned dramatically.

"I—"

"Did you see the hurt in their eyes?" she interrupted. "For heaven's sake, they are pitifully eager to please you. And if they manage it, *God help them*, they shall end up bored and boring. Just like *you!*"

"Good!" He paced toward the fountain's large stone fountain and then turned. "Better bored and boring like me than lying and stealing one's way through the countryside like you. For the last time, Miss Jones, my children are not to be indulging in silly fairy stories. I am ordering you: do not tell them any such stories, and do not encourage them to create them!" He growled.

She walked right up to him, put her hands on her hips, and scowled up at him. "I will tell those sweet little girls stories whenever I wish. And I do not care if you dismiss me!"

"Good. I will do that as soon as possible."

"Good. In the meantime, I will do whatever *I* think is right!"

"I detest needing you." He sneered.

"I detest that you need me." She sneered right back.

"There's a kissing bough above our heads."

"Yes."

"I detest kissing boughs."

"Good."

"I am going to kiss you now."

"Fine!"

And then he kissed her.

He pulled her against him, enclosing her in the cocoon of his embrace, shutting out the world and all conscious thought. His arms were strong, his body solid, and the scent of him filled her nostrils. His mouth was unexpectedly soft as it quested against hers, and she melted against him like a late spring snow and kissed him back.

After what might have been a second or an hour

—Emily couldn't have told—he grasped her shoulders and set her away from him.

Blinking once, twice, he gave his waistcoat a downward tug before taking a swipe at his errant curls.

"Yes," he said. "Well then."

"Well," she said. "Fine."

"Good," he murmured.

"Indeed."

And then they kissed again.

If Emily's emotions were swirling before, now they were a blizzard. *I cannot believe this is happening!* she thought. Afraid that if she opened her eyes, she'd find it was all just a dream, she risked a peek —only to discover that Baby was standing right behind the Viscount!

10

BABY IS DISCOVERED

*E*MILY FROZE, REALIZING too late that when a lady is kissing a gentleman and the lady stops quite suddenly, the gentleman tends to notice. The Viscount had, and again he broke their kiss.

Behind him, Baby waved a pilfered bouquet joyously about.

Emily *had* to distract the Viscount! There was only one thing to do. Grasping the lapels of his coat, she pulled him to her and kissed him with what could be described more as zeal than passion, and this time, her eyes were open.

Wide open.

He responded to her wanton kiss. *La*, did he respond!

As they kissed, Emily took one step backward. And another. And still another, hoping to draw him outside of the glasshouse, and it was working beautifully! The trouble was, her ploy was also working on Baby, who was matching them step for step.

She groaned with frustration.

He groaned with ... something else.

At that moment, Baby lost interest in her tatty bouquet. And a normal, happy, active baby elephant just *has* to find *something* to do with her busy little trunk.

She found something. She found the Viscount's hair!

Her questing little trunk, with its three finger-like appendages, got busy exploring his bouncy, wayward curls.

The Viscount kissed Emily harder.

Then, apparently tiring of his hair, Baby turned to his ear.

The Viscount groaned and kissed her even more ardently. "Oh, Miss Jones!"

Baby's restless trunk moved on—only to caress his neck ... his shoulder ... and then down his back—

"Ah, Miss Jones ... Emily!"

—until she was drawing careless circles on—

"Your bottom!" Emily thrust herself away from him.

"Yes," he drawled. "You expected to find someone else's back there, perhaps?"

"My Lord Winter!"

"Miss Jones?"

"My Lord Winter!"

"Miss Jones!" He chuckled.

"Oh, la! My lord! It was not me!"

"Oh?" He was laughing now.

"It was ... it was—" She closed her eyes. "My lord ... it was my elephant."

He wheeled around, which was definitely an imprudent thing to do, for now Baby's trunk was situated one hundred and eighty degrees opposite of where it had been, through no fault of her own. Lord Winter danced away, sputtering. "That is an— an elephant," he managed to wheeze out after a moment that felt like an eternity.

"Yes, my lord," Emily said in a pained voice, "it is my elephant."

"Your *elephant? Your* elephant? Yours? *Yours?* How can it be *your deuced elephant?!*" He punctuated each syllable with an outward thrust of his index finger through the air. "Wait!" he cried before she could think of anything to say. "Oh, God! I remember now. That sound! The sound we heard as we returned to Stendmore Park yesterday. A sound like a trumpet! I thought it sounded like an elephant, but I dismissed that idea out of hand. It was too ridiculous!" he cried and then repeated her words to him. *"'I brought with me an elephant and have been secretly keeping it out in your stable.'* Dear God, you were telling the truth!"

Emily took a deep breath. Now was not the time to panic. "She was being mistreated, you see," she began, "so I rescued her." And out tumbled the entire story of the sad, traveling menagerie she'd come across two days before arriving at Stendmore Park, an ancient, toothless monkey, a snake, a nearly featherless ostrich, and the poor baby elephant.

Lord Winter listened calmly, considering that an elephant was standing next to him, ripping apart and tasting plant matter the entire time Emily talked. If Baby liked whatever species it was, it was loudly and enthusiastically consumed, and if she did not like it, it was enthusiastically waved about before it was even more enthusiastically tossed aside. Oh, yes, Baby was having a grand time!

Emily was not.

The longer she talked, the angrier the Viscount appeared.

"And they just let you take her?" he finally burst out.

"Well ... no ..."

"So you took her without asking them? Just like that? Are you *mad*? You cannot just go about the countryside pilfering pachyderms whenever the mood strikes!"

"It wasn't like that."

"Oh? I suppose you *planned* to take it, then? You awakened that morning and said to yourself, 'Emily, my girl, today is a lovely day to relieve someone of his elephant!'"

"It wasn't like that, either," she said stubbornly. "I had no other choice."

"No other choice? You could have left it right where it was! Instead, you followed one of your bacon-brained impulses and landed us both in high seas! What did you imagine you were going to do with her once you'd spirited her away? What will you do with her when you leave here? And how can I convince everyone I've changed with a stolen baby elephant in my house?"

Emily stilled, blinking. "Is *that* what this house

party is about? You trying to convince the neighborhood you are no longer a rakehell?"

He shoved back the curl that always seemed to be astray. "There is more to it than that," he said. "Much more." Looking suddenly tired, he put his fists to his temples wiped them across his face and sighing heavily. The truth is I am destitute, and the Prince would love to see my title and estate reabsorbed."

"Ah yes, the infamous peacock feather and the duchess incident!"

"How do you know about that?" he demanded.

"One of the servants," she averred, neglecting to tell him she'd overheard one of her servants back in London gossiping about it and that the woman had clamped her lips shut as soon as Emily approached, so that the details had remained tantalizingly out of reach.

"I should not be surprised."he said. "There probably isn't a person in the Kingdom who doesn't know about that episode and a thousand others, real or imagined. I earned the reputation I have. But, devil take it, my children did not! And this house party is my last hope for them."

So it was as Emily suspected. "You hope to prove to everyone—Mrs. Kellerman, the good doctor, the parson, all your neighbors and even your own servants that you have changed."

He nodded.

"Why is that so important?" she asked. "Why should you care what they think? If they are so blind they cannot see that you are a good man, a kind man —"

"I hope to secure loans from my guests in order to bring the estate back from the brink."

"Oh. I see."

"But no one will make me a loan if they find I have *blasted stolen baby elephant* in my house! Most of these people have never even seen an elephant. They have never been to London. Most of them have never traveled further than the next village. They live in a world that never changes, where anything out of the ordinary is discussed over and over for years. They will find it shocking. They will take it as evidence — outrageous evidence! — that I am the same as I always was. That I have been playing them for fools. Do you know what they would if they find I have a stolen elephant hidden away in my house?"

"She is not in your house, she is in your glasshouse, and I did not steal her. I bought her with a ring my grandmother gave me." Emily's eyes pricked with tears. That ring had been important to her, but not as important as saving Baby had been. "I just did not tell the owners that I was buying her, that is all."

"You did not even *ask* if they wanted to sell her!" He growled. "You are outside of enough! Leap and the net will appear! Seize the day, *carpe diem!* Just like my children! Just like—"

"Just like you," she interrupted. "The real you."

He waved one exasperated hand in the air. "You cannot possibly know what I am like!" Once more, he pushed that endearing lock of hair off of his forehead.

"You are just like that hair of yours," she said. "You cannot be tamed. It's just not in your nature."

"My nature, *Miss Net-Shall-Appear*, is to be responsible, cautious, and controlled!" he said in a frantic tone that suggested just the opposite.

"Oh? Then why did you kiss me just now?"

His face registered shock, but then he clamped his lips together and shook his head.

She grinned. "Oh, *la!* I just figured it out!"

"What?" he demanded. "What did you 'figure out?'"

"That you are afraid of yourself!"

"What buffleheaded nonsense are you spouting now?"

"You have tried hard to bury it, but it surfaces unbidden," she went on, as though he hadn't spoken. "All of it. The spontaneity, the joy. The sarcasm, the irreverence. And the purely human desire to share those things with others. You are no different from anyone else—even though you fancy yourself an automaton!"

"You go too far," he said, his voice rigid with anger.

"No, my Lord Winter, I do not go far enough! And I'd best speak my mind before you have me banished." She pulled herself up to her full height. "You can suppress those human qualities in yourself if you wish, but you have no right to try to turn your little children into automatons as your own parents tried to do to you!"

"Pack your bags," he said. "You are leaving."

"I have no bags," she said and turned to go. "Come, Baby."

As though the elephant understood her, she wrapped her trunk around Emily's wrist and walked toward the door behind her. It was cold outside.

~

"Oh, God," David groaned behind them. "Stop!"

Miss Jones stopped but did not turn around. "Yes, my lord?"

He could see her watching him in the reflection of the glass. He ran a hand through his hair. "You cannot go."

"That is not a very good apology, my lord."

He sighed. "You are right. And I was wrong. Again. Miss Jones, you seem to bring out the worst in me. Please stay."

"Thank you, my lord. Well done. I will stay of course—since I have no other place to go."

"And yet you would have walked away from here."

"Indeed."

He sighed. "What am I to do with you?"

"Well, since you shall have to wed an heiress if you cannot convince Mrs. Kellerman and her ilk that you are a paragon of respectability, I suppose kissing me again is out of the question?"

"Unfortunately," he said with a wry smile. "Miss Jones, we need to talk about the whole kissing business."

"I do not agree," she said. "I think we both know all there is to know about the 'whole kissing business.' Don't you?"

Even in the moonlight, David could see her skin flush. Oh, yes, they both knew all there was to know about why they'd kissed. What they did not know is how much more there could be between them. How it would feel to go on kissing, uninterrupted, perhaps in his bedchamber ... in his bed ... with nothing between them but a whisper ...

David shook himself.

She pulled the edges of her cloak closed in front of her. "I think you had better write me a letter of recommendation forthwith. I will use the time until Miss Bull returns to secure a position elsewhere."

"And your elephant?"

Miss Jones pasted on a serious expression. "She is unskilled, I am afraid. And you cannot send her out into the cold. Not without a sweater, lunch, and pocket money."

He smiled a little and then sobered. "Be serious."

"Could she not stay here? Please?"

He sighed. "I suppose Mr. Sneed is aware of her presence?"

She hesitated.

"Speak," David said and held up one palm. "I promise he will receive no punishment. Not even a set-down. He helped me hide many animals when I was a boy, and I knew even then it wasn't for my benefit but for theirs. I revered him for it, and it would be hypocritical indeed for me to punish him now for the same offense."

She gave him a warm smile. "In that case, he is quite aware."

And you are too attractive, David thought. *Blast!* She wasn't at all the sort of female David needed or wanted. She was too forthright, too impulsive, and too poor. The sooner she left Stendmore Park, the better.

"Good night," he said with a bow and beat a hasty retreat before he kissed her again.

"ORGIVE ME, MY lord," one of David's footmen-on-duty said. "I have tried asking them to come back later, but they refuse to leave until they have seen you."

David slid from his bed and wiped his eyes. "Tell them to wait in my study—and keep an eye on them," he added as the footman turned to go. Apparently, three visitors had arrived. Two rough-looking men and a boy. He looked at the mantel clock and groaned. It wasn't even eight-o'-the-clock yet. He'd been abed only five hours.

David dressed carelessly, intending to go back to sleep for another hour or two after he saw Whoever-They-Were. Probably some creditors of Robert's. With any luck, they'd be the run-of-the-mill sort. Unpaid glovers or tailors. Fishmongers. Haymen. Any sort of debt was better than a gambling debt. Nothing could be worse than that, he thought.

But he was wrong.

The men were there to demand their elephant back.

"Elephant?" David calmly repeated.

"We knows you have it," said one. Tall, pale, and gaunt, the man held his cap respectfully before him in his dirty hands, but his expression didn't look respectful. "It was taken from our camp in the middle of the night. A bauble was left as payment, but it ain't enough. Not by half. We wants more."

"Much more," the shorter man added. "We can prove the elephant's ours. Unless you have a bill of sale," he said.

"*We* have one," the taller man said, patting his pocket. "So we can prove it's ours. And you've got it. We seen it down there in your glasshouse."

David's brow slammed together. How long had these two had been roving over his land? Spying and poking about with his two little girls and Miss Jones traipsing about unescorted and unprotected?

David stood and leaned menacingly over his desk. "We deal harshly with trespassers in this part of the country, a thing you ... *gentlemen* would be well advised to remember."

"We wants our elephant," said the short man. "We won it, fair and square."

"That's right," said his companion before launching into a story about how they'd encountered the elephant in London just as it was being unloaded from a ship Ceylon. Then, they'd apparently gambled for the elephant and won.

David didn't believe a word of it. He didn't know the real story behind their acquisition of an elephant, but he had stopped listening, for the boy standing behind them, silent and eyes averted, told David all he needed to know.

David knew a servant from a slave. On his travels with the English Navy, he'd seen both. He'd seen beloved, well-cared-for slaves and neglected servants. Neither especially aroused his sympathy. But this little boy was dressed for a winter in Ceylon, not a winter in England. He had nothing but a shabby cloak to keep him warm. He was pitifully thin. And, worst of all, he flinched whenever the men moved too suddenly. Anger tightened David's chest.

"It is snowing outside. How will you keep the elephant warm?" David asked.

"That's our concern," the skinny man answered.

David clenched his jaws together and then demanded, "Show me the ring."

The men traded cold, calculating looks. "What ring?" said the first.

"The bauble you mentioned."

"Oh. That." he shifted. "'Twas but a beat-up old half-crown. We don't have no ring."

"In that case," said David, "*my* elephant cannot possibly belong to you, for the ring was left as payment for her. Good day."

"All right ... what if we *did* have a ring?" the other man said. "It still wouldn't be near enough to compensate us for losing the elephant."

David smiled a smile that did not reach his eyes. "Gentlemen, I intend to keep *my* elephant. Let us settle on a fair price."

Five minutes later, the men left the house with half of David's remaining silver. David tucked the bill of sale into his coat pocket and bade the little boy follow him to the warm kitchen.

Cook, bless her, didn't bat an eyelash. One look at the brown-skinned boy and she pulled her own shawl from a peg and wrapped it about his thin shoulders. "Are you hungry, my dear? Of course you are!" she said, reaching for a bowl and spoon.

There was porridge on the stove, and David didn't doubt there would soon be some in the boy's stomach. Porridge and whatever else Cook could muster.

David barked an order to a maid to fetch Miss Jones and headed for the glasshouse. He hadn't gone very far, however, when the little boy came running up along behind him.

"Sahib!" the boy cried. "Are you finding the elephant now? I will go with you," he said, and David saw that his hands clung to his steaming bowl of porridge, which was obviously too hot. David pulled his cravat from his neck and helped the boy wrap the bowl in the rumpled linen. "Thank you, Sahib."

"My name is David Stendmore, the Viscount Winter. What is your name?"

"I am Rohan, Davidstendmore," said the boy.

David smiled in spite of his state of agitation. "I suppose you want to go see your elephant, Rohan?"

"Yes, Davidstendmore."

"This way. Slowly, now. That porridge is hot. Wouldn't want you to burn your fingers. Would you like me to carry it?"

"No, Davidstendmore. I shall carry. Rohan is strong," the boy said proudly.

David wrapped his hand around the boy's thin arm and gave his weak muscles a little squeeze. "You *are* strong—just like a chickadee!" David said, and little Rohan beamed, because, as David had assumed, he had no idea what a 'chickadee' was. David chuckled, but then he looked toward the glasshouse and sobered.

"Good morning!" Miss Jones called behind them, just emerging from the house. David waited for her to catch up to them. "Who have we here?" She smiled at the boy. Obviously, she did not recognize him.

"This is Rohan. He is the elephant's mahout."

"La!" Miss Jones looked wildly about them.

"No, no!" David reassured her. "There is no danger. I took care of everything." He explained about the visitors as they walked to the glasshouse, which was set quite a distance from the main house, thank God. One could just see the top of the glasshouse peeking over the tall yew hedges that surrounded it, and it was cold enough outside that none of his guests would be willing to walk that far.

"… and then Rohan and I had a little chat after they left," he continued. "Back in Ceylon, he and his elephant were destined to stay together their whole lives, but then they were both abducted and sold into slavery a few months ago. They were brought to London against their will, and the men you took her from apparently won her from the new owner, who was gambling while foxed. They had a proper bill of sale, though."

"A proper bill of sale!" she cried. "You are not going to give those poor, defenseless darlings back to those —"

"Not to worry! I told you. I took care of everything. I own Baby now." David pulled the paper from his pocket. "I have a legal bill of sale. She is safe. They both are."

Miss Jones's shoulders slumped in relief, and tears welled in her eyes. She turned away and wiped her face. David's irritation subsided a little in the face of her compassion. However harebrained her reasoning had been when she'd stolen the elephant, it was clear her heart had been in the right place.

The boy wasn't paying them any attention. Instead, he was peering through the door of the glasshouse and into its overgrown foliage, attempting to spot his elephant. "Laleeta!" he cried, finally catching sight of her. "Laleeta!" He ran inside, and David and Miss Jones followed him.

Baby trumpeted in recognition and rushed up to Rohan, her trunk extended. He wrapped his arms about her neck, and with her trunk, the elephant gave him what could only be described as a hug before she ran off in the opposite direction, clearly daring him to chase her. They dashed off toward the opposite side of the enormous glasshouse.

"Thank you," Miss Jones said, looking up at David with shining eyes that almost tempted him into feeling proud. Feeling glad that he'd traded the bulk of his remaining silver for a baby elephant and a bedraggled little boy.

"Buying her and freeing the boy was a good and generous thing to do," she said.

"It was an impulsive and stupid thing to do, and I am certain I shall regret it," he countered.

"Nonsense. Everything has been settled admirably."

"What?" He threw her an incredulous look. "*Nothing* has been settled. What am I to do with a little boy and an elephant?"

"You should have thought about that before you bought them," Miss Jones said with a mischievous grin.

He should have been irritated with her. Hell, he should have been livid. But then she looked at him that way, and all he could think about was kissing her again.

David looked away. "I suppose I shall have to keep Baby Laleeta and Rohan here at Stendmore Park until the spring, when I can send them back home to Ceylon as long as it is safe to do so."

Instantly, joy blossomed on her face. "Oh! I was hoping you would say so!"

"You must promise to keep her secret until the house party is over with."

"Of course."

"This time of year and especially with snow on the ground, there is little danger of my guests wandering about the grounds. It should be easy to keep her secret." David went on before she could answer. "After the house party, I shall let it be known that I ordered the elephant as a gift for my children." He sighed and waved his hand toward the house. "They will all think it outlandish behavior, but it will be *my* outlandish behavior, not my children's, and by that time I will have received my loans."

"Rohan and his parents will so happy to be reunited!"

David shook his head. "Unfortunately he is an orphan."

"Oh, poor little boy!" Her face folded into lines of concern. "We cannot send them back to Ceylon if there is no one to watch over them. They will not be safe."

"I know that, silly girl." He chucked her under the chin with a smile. "I am not entirely heartless. If I cannot find a safe place for the boy and his elephant, then the logical, inevitable, damnable conclusion is that Rohan and Laleeta will have to stay here—and I will always be *The Viscount with the Elephant*." He frowned. "But if that is the only outrageous thing that ever happens around here, and if I live a life that is otherwise entirely unremarkable and respectable, then I suppose that in time I can live it down."

"Oh, my lord Winter! You are a good and kind man!" She looked like she was about to launch herself into his arms and kiss him, and part of him wished she would, but somehow he found the power to take a small step back from her, and the moment was lost. *No more kissing.* He should never have kissed her in the first place. He'd had no right.

And he'd better find something else to think of.

He looked down and stuck his hand into his pocket. "The scoundrels who owned Baby also gave me this." He took the ring from his pocket and held it out to her.

"My grandmother's ring!" she cried. "They did

not '*give*' you this. You must have bargained for it, and I know you have little money, so what did you trade?"

"It is yours." He ignored her question. "Take it."

"I cannot. Not before I pay you back."

"Yes. You must." He straightened and tried to look stern. "I am your employer, Miss Jones, and I command it. Consider it an advance on your wages. Or a Christmas bonus."

"Well, in that case," —she dimpled and curtsied — "yes, my lord. If I must." She held out her left hand, palm down, her glee belying her protest. "Grandmama always wore it on her index finger, but it fits better on my ring finger," she said.

David swallowed. The silly chit actually expected him to place the blasted ring—a heart-shaped diamond, no less!—on her finger!

She wrinkled her adorable pink nose. "Did you know that Mary Queen of Scots sent her sister a ring with a heart-shaped diamond on it? Grandmama told me it was taken as a symbol of friendship ever after—though I cannot imagine why, as we all know how *that* ended." She laughed, and David slipped the heart-shaped diamond onto her slender hand.

Just like in a wedding ceremony.

He'd been married once before, of course, but he had not loved Rebecca. She was a sweet and biddable thing and not unintelligent, but she'd been common and rough, and he'd married her as much to displease his parents as he had to rescue her.

What would it feel like to stand beside someone he truly loved? To pledge undying love to a woman who challenged him, enjoyed his company, and loved him back?

He wondered if Emily were wondering the same thing.

Madness.

He had to stop this. He had to stop it all right now. He had to apologize for kissing her. He had to tell her it meant nothing. That it was just the mistletoe, the moonlight, the moment. "Miss Jones ... last night, I—"

"*La*, it was only a silly kiss!" she said. "I hardly fancy we are the first pair to be gripped by a sudden, momentary passion." She stretched out her left hand to admire the ring.

"Momentary?"

"Indeed. I am, as you pointed out, much too spontaneous. It is I who should apologize. I am the one who hung the kissing bough out here. The girls could not wait until Christmas Eve to hang some greenery, and I could see no harm in it. Hanging greenery before Christmas cannot in truth be bad luck out here."

"We kissed because of it," he reminded her.

"Yes, we did," she agreed.

"And that was not a lucky thing," he said.

"No," she agreed. "It *was* unlucky, I daresay."

"Then we are in agreement?" he asked.

"I believe we are," she answered.

"It was just a momentary passion, then," he said.

"Yes …"

"A passing ephemera."

"Indeed."

He couldn't help it. His gaze flicked down to her lips. "The kissing bough is still there."

"It is."

"And the boy is at the far end of the glasshouse cavorting with Baby."

"I hear them."

"Which means I could kiss you again, and no one would know."

"It does."

"And I want to."

"Good."

"Fine, then."

And, for the second time in twelve hours, David

found himself kissing his children's blasted governess!

She broke the kiss first and stepped back from him, eyes wide. Pointing up to the kissing bough, she said, "I shall remove the thing forthwith."

"Please do. And pray do not hang any more."

"Heaven forbid!"

He spun on his heel and left, and Emily stood staring after him, feeling she might shatter into a thousand pieces and blow away. What was this madness? What was she doing kissing the Viscount again? What if they were discovered? There would be no escaping the parson's mousetrap—and she'd be stuck with Lord Winter for all eternity. She was here trying to *avoid* marriage, not to be trapped into one! *Dear heaven!* She didn't want a man who sneered at play and scowled at levity. Lord Winter was entirely too deliberate, too controlled, too rigid.

And entirely much too tempting. A tempting enigma.

He was a man who rescued baby elephants and children in need, who laughed at snowballs tossed down harridans' necklines! But at the same time, he was trying to convince everyone he had abandoned that sort of behavior. And he was trying to convince himself he'd changed even harder than he was trying to convince the neighborhood. What if he were successful? What if he managed to transform himself into the person he thought he should be?

The point was moot anyway, Emily told herself. For she wasn't what he'd want in a wife. And even if Lord Winter suddenly lost his ordered, plodding, calculating, unbending mind and decided he wanted a wife of Emily's temperament, Emily just couldn't risk it. She didn't want a husband like him—no matter how endearing his rare smiles or how hard her toes curled when he kissed her.

Behind her she heard rustling and turned to see Baby and her little mahout come forward through the thick, un-tended growth of the shrubbery.

"This is like the forest in my land," he said with a grin. "It will be very good for hiding."

"Hiding?"

"Sahib says it is my task to keep Laleeta hidden."

"Is that her name? Laleeta?"

"Yes. It means 'play' in my language."

Emily laughed. The name was certainly apt.

"Your name is Rohan?" At his nod she asked, "Does it have a special meaning, too?"

"In Hindi, it means 'ascending,'" he said proudly. But then his little brown face wrinkled up in uncertain lines. "I am wondering, can ma'am sahib tell me if in coming here I have ascended or *de*scended?"

She laughed. "I am afraid I do not know, Rohan, for I am still trying to answer that question for myself!"

"Hullo!" Mr. Sneed called from the door of the glasshouse. "We wondered where you were."

"We?"

Rose and Rain appeared from behind the old stable master. "The girls came down to the stable looking for you. I wanted to know if they can help me make over a horse blanket for Baby." Mr. Sneed spied Rohan. "And who is this?"

Emily made the proper introductions, and Mr. Sneed explained to her that he'd transferred Baby Laleeta into the glasshouse at around midnight because he'd worried that the stable was too cold. "It's cold enough in here, as it is."

"Sahib is wise," the little boy said and looked worried. "Elephant children sicken and die if they are not kept warm."

Cries of dismay rent the air.

"What if it snows again, Miss Jones?" Rain said.

"What if it gets too cold?" Rose moaned. "Oh, our Baby must be kept warm!"

"But how?" Mr. Sneed said. "We can't take a chance on her kicking over a brazier in here and burning the place down, and she ain't going to climb up the ladder into my place over the coach house."

"She could stay in the nursery," Rain said.

Rose snorted. "We cannot bring her into the house, silly. Papa would be cross."

"I can help her up the stairs," Rohan said proudly.

"How else are we to keep her warm?" Rain asked.

"How indeed?" Emily murmured, chewing her lip. Peering up through the roof of the glasshouse, she could just make out the nursery windows. *How indeed?*

Outside the glasshouse, Ophelia Robertson chuckled.

"Shh!" warned her friend Griselda. "They will hear you!"

"It is no matter," said Ophelia and turned back toward the great, sprawling house. She had only just arrived an hour ago when a footman had taken her up to see Lady Griselda, who was awaiting her arrival. They'd been hovering in the hall near Lord Winter's study while he was talking to his visitors, and they'd ducked into the morning room just in time for him to miss them as he'd stormed off to the kitchen with the little boy in tow. They'd followed him to the glasshouse and had seen and heard everything. "I have seen all I needed to see and hear," Ophelia said. "I know exactly what must be done."

Though she didn't know either of the young people in question personally, she'd known *of* them for years. Ophelia knew *everyone* worth knowing.

She knew their parents, too. Both sets. Odious creatures, the lot of them. But their children, by some trick of fate, had turned out fine. A little too rebellious, a little too wild, perhaps, but that just meant they were a fine match for each other.

If she could help them see it for themselves.

"Do you think you can bring them together?"

"Well, of course I can, my dear Griselda! But first, I must prepare myself."

"For what?"

"For a nap!" Ophelia cackled. "Nothing will be done until tonight. Then I shall make my move."

"What are you planning?"

"To ruin the Viscount's house party."

Her friend gasped. "Oh, my! How? Why?"

Ophelia chuckled again. "Your little friend is planning to smuggle her elephant up to the nursery, I think."

Griselda nodded. "That much seems clear."

"And nurseries have doors on them."

"Yes, but, what has that to do with—"

"Lord Winter has rescued Miss Jones. I believe it is her turn to rescue him."

"Whatever do you mean?" demanded Griselda.

"Your young friend is clever and in love, and I know exactly what *I* would do in her situation. Or, rather," —Ophelia cackled— "the situation in which she will find herself this evening."

"Ophelia, you worry me. I begin to wonder if calling for your assistance was the right thing to do."

"Just wait and see, my dear." Ophelia smiled. "Wait and see."

12

DISASTER

*C*HRISTMAS EVE DAWNED clear and cold. The temperature dropped steadily all day, until the wind began to howl and a relentless, swirling snow covered everything in a tempest of white. But David barely noticed what was going on outside, for inside, Miss Jones was busy turning his household upside down.

She'd appeared with the children downstairs just after breakfast, declaring that the holiday was one time when it was right and proper for children to take part—indeed, without them there would be something lacking! David was horrified at first, but when the guests remarked upon his children's pretty manners and congratulated him on finding such an effective new governess, David relaxed—until he discovered that the guests were hanging kissing boughs all over the house!

Somehow, Miss Jones had taken charge of the decorating, and she'd been commanding the servants—and even the guests—like Nelson his fleet. They'd hung miles and miles of greenery and paper flowers about the ancient great hall. She'd enlisted the elders to cut foil stars and red silk flowers, and the young people were balanced atop chairs and tables hanging the blasted things and laughing. Those not otherwise involved were singing or playing the pianoforte. The servants had already broken out bottles of Mr. Sneed's cottage ale, and, though the mistletoe in the servants' hall was already devoid of berries, no one paid any attention and the continued stolen kisses were the source of much muted laughter coming from the direction of the kitchen and servants' hall.

The world had gone mad.

Was this the way Christmas celebrations always were? He supposed so. Still, it was unsettling. His only comfort was that the guests didn't seem to think anything was out of the ordinary. In fact, Mrs. Kellerman had declared the evening to be "a paragon of good taste and refinement!" The entire drawing room was buzzing with it.

And so, amidst the ritual Christmas chaos, David tried to relax. All was well. His guests were happy. Rose and Rain were calmly playing spillikins on the floor of the drawing room. Miss Jones was smiling. The elephant was nowhere to be seen. Everything was proceeding as he'd planned.

He ought to feel happy, David told himself.

Though the Viscount and the governess stood at opposite ends of the room—as far away from the kissing boughs as they could—they were both trying to convince themselves of the same thing.

She ought to feel happy, Emily told herself.

The day had been a complete success. Indeed, the entire journey—*her* journey—had been a complete success. She'd avoided being endlessly pushed toward the Duke of Besshire for an entire, blissful month. She'd become a governess, easily tarnishing her reputation enough to discourage all but the most ardent or avaricious of suitors. And she could cause her parents enough humiliation that they would give up their campaign to force her to marry altogether and allow her to settle into a life of contented, unwed, country rustication.

On top of that, she'd made new friends. Children, servants, country gentry, and an elephant! It had been an adventure. She'd leapt and the net had appeared. It had been glorious.

And it wasn't over. Not if she didn't want it to be.

Two letters had arrived that afternoon. One was from Miss Bull. Her mother had recovered, and she would be returning in a few days. Though she hinted that her mother's health was tenuous, and it might be time for her to retire. Miss Bull hadn't tendered her resignation, though, and the Viscount hadn't offered Emily a permanent position.

The other letter was an answer to an advertisement the Viscount had helped her place in several newspapers. If her parents would not see reason and let her escape into the country, she could threaten them with the letter—or she could make good on that threat and in truth continue on as a governess!

Everything would have been perfect if she hadn't been faced with the fact that her next assignment would not include the Hellions or Baby Laleeta or darling little Rohan. And neither would it include her blasted employer, with whom she'd fallen in love like a silly mooncalf. Even now, the mixed-up man was trying his best to look like he wasn't interested in the festivities, whereas any fool could see he was about to burst with the desire to join in.

Shortly before nine-o'-the-clock, as she stood staring into the flames slowly consuming the enormous Yule log, he found her. With a house full of guests, it was the first time she'd had a moment to herself.

"It is about time for the children to retire, is it not?" he asked quietly. No one was nearby, and they could speak without being overheard.

"Yes." She nodded toward where the girls sat, playing with the set of ivory spillikins Gertie had given them. Little Rohan was upstairs in the nursery under strict instructions to stay there with Baby Laleeta and keep her quiet. "I hate to make them go to bed, but they have had a long day, and they are tired, I am certain."

"They have had a grand time today."

She smiled. "So have I." And she meant it. It had

been the best Christmas Eve she'd ever had. "I will herd them upstairs when their game is finished."

"You *will* come back downstairs, will you not?" he asked.

She looked over at the children. "It is a governess's task to keep watch over them. I could not ask anyone else to watch them. Not tonight."

"I daresay they will be fast asleep in no time. Once they're out, you can leave them and return to check on them once in awhile. Please say you will come to supper," he begged quietly. "I have no doubt you are responsible, in part, for my impending success. I would like you to be there at the pivotal moment, when I finally ask and receive pledges for the loans I seek."

He was too appealing. She shook her head. "I cannot."

"Of course you can," said a voice behind them. It was Mrs. Ophelia Robertson, a latecomer to the house party. She was apparently supposed to have arrived with Sir Basil and Lady Griselda, as a sort of companion to the Lady, but she had been delayed. "You *must* come to supper, my dear, Your charges will be asleep. Winter, you must help me convince her!" she batted the Viscount with her fan. "A governess does not belong in the servants' hall on an occasion like this. She is never fully accepted there. On special occasions, she must be invited to dine with the family. It is the proper thing to do. You would not want to be considered *im*proper, would you?" And with that, she sailed off across the drawing room.

"No," Lord Winter said to her back. "I would not." He turned to Emily. "You heard the lady. Please say you will attend."

She lowered her eyes. "I will be there."

And she was.

She was there when he stood up at the head of the supper table to confess his past sins. When he expressed his regret for his wild, misspent youth. When he asked his neighbors to forgive him for bringing scorn upon Buxley-on-Isis. When he explained that he'd worked hard to reform and that he intended to continue working for the good of the neighborhood until the end of his days. And she was there when he finally asked for his loans.

She was there when Mrs. Kellerman, the harridan, declared publicly that she'd been watching Lord Winter for signs of being a wastrel but that she'd found none. "In fact," Mrs. Kellerman said, "I believe he has changed completely. I would not have believed it, but he is as stiff and sober as a gravestone. No adventures. No high jinks—except those instigated by others." She glared at Emily before continuing. "He has nothing to hide, and Mr. Kellerman and I will be happy to pledge a loan in the amount of five thousand pounds. I am sure that if our neighbors will do the same—each to the extent of his own ability, of course," she said, knowing full well there wasn't one family in Buxley who could pledge half so much and obviously enjoying the knowledge immensely, "I am certain Stendmore Park will prosper. With the proper management and supervision from the investors, of course."

And Emily was also there when Baby Laleeta (having escaped from the nursery with a little help from Ophelia Robertson, unbeknownst to everyone but Laleeta herself), smelling the food and the drink, charged into the dining room trumpeting and swinging her trunk and reaching for the tray of syllabubs.

David gasped.

All hell broke loose.

Most of his guests screamed. Two fainted. He

watched as the blasted elephant grabbed the tall, footed, silver syllabub tray and tipped it, sending its frothy contents cascading over Dr. Brown and from there onto the floor. Sir Basil's dogs, who had been asleep in front of the fire in the drawing room, rushed into the dining room to investigate the ruckus, barking and whining. The elephant ran around the table trying to avoid them. Half the guests scrambled to stand, sliding in the syllabub and colliding, and the other half cowered under the table.

Miss Jones tried to herd Baby Laleeta out the door, but the elephant, apparently reassured by her presence, only made a mad grab for a cup of syllabub that sat on the table. This time, she was successful, and the syllabub made its splashing, dribbling way into her pink mouth. But it was a pitifully small amount for an elephant, and she quickly discarded the syllabub glass with a crystalline shatter and reached for another.

Into the melee charged Rose and Rain, followed by the little mahout, who was shouting in Hindi.

The only person not standing or prone was Mrs. Kellerman, who, imperious, still sat at the dining table, looking as though she smelled something bad —until Baby reached for *her* glass of syllabub, and the old harpy tried to snatch it back. It slipped, flew into the air, and David watched as, seemingly in slow motion, the trumpet-shaped syllabub glass tumbled against Mrs. Kellerman's expansive chest, the syllabub flowing between her bosoms.

Baby saved the situation by plunging her trunk into the lady's *décolletage* and loudly slurping the concoction.

Mrs. Kellerman let out a bloodcurdling scream, and into the shocked silence that followed, Emily Jones dealt the final, crushing, killing blow.

"Lord Winter did not know about my Baby! I swear it!"

"You have an infant, *Miss* Jones?" The harridan sneered, having savagely batted Baby's trunk away.

Everyone—apart from Mrs. Ophelia Robertson, who had, only just come back from the lady's retiring room, and was, inexplicably, smiling broadly—was suddenly staring at Emily, their mouths open, and Emily realized what she'd said. "No!" she cried "Oh, no! That is not what I meant! It is not my baby. It is *his*."

"*Well!*" Mrs. Kellerman blustered ",Just how long have you employed this ... this *governess*, Lord Winter?"

Emily blanched. "No! That is not what I meant, either!"

Most of the company averted their gazes, and Emily looked to Lord Winter, whose expression registered dismay, defeat, and despair as the horrible scene coalesced and began its journey into local legend.

13

NOTHING TO LOSE

*E*LEPHANTS WERE NOT the only ones who never forgot.

It didn't matter what Emily said now. Nothing she could do would repair the damage she'd done. Her heart broke in two. Because of her, everything was ruined. But—*oh, la!*—she couldn't just sit there and not try! She had to do *something*. *Say* something. But she hadn't the first notion what.

Several servants had hurried in when the commotion broke out. They now stood frozen in place like everyone else. Then, as though on cue, they all began to move at once. Gertie ushered the girls out of the dining room and up the stairs. Rohan ushered the elephant over to a corner and tried to look invisible. Several footmen stood at the ready with towels, obviously waiting for *someone* to give them the word to tidy up. In a moment, life would go on at Stendmore Park, but it would proceed along a very different vector than it would have, had Emily never come. She had to do something. Anything.

With one last, impulsive leap into the unknown, Emily opened her mouth to speak. "My name," she began, "isn't Emily Jones, and I am not in truth the governess. My name is Miss Emily Winthrop, and if you need proof, Sir Basil and Lady Griselda can confirm that."

The pair nodded solemnly as the harridan blustered. "Emily *Winthrop!* Not Miss Emily Winthrop of Windlay Square?"

"The very same!" chimed Mrs. Robertson. "I see word of her disappearance has echoed even here."

"I beg your pardon!" Mrs. Kellerman turned to address Mrs. Robertson with an acid expression. "Buxley-on-Isis is a perfectly respectable village of adequate size. It is *not* some *backwater*, Mrs...."

"Robertson. You have not been to London much, have you, my dear?"

Emily winced.

Mrs. Kellerman sniffed. "This is *not* London, Madam."

"No," Mrs. Robertson said dryly. "It is not."

Mrs. Kellerman didn't back down. Instead, she seemed even more incensed as she turned to the Viscount. "Do you mean to tell me, Lord Winter, that you have been harboring a runaway heiress under your roof? Un-chaperoned?"

"An heiress?" the Viscount drawled. "It would seem so." His deep, brown eyes, which had been sparkling with anticipation and promise earlier in the evening, were now dull and dark, and the pieces of Emily's heart were crushed.

"Humph!" Mrs. Kellerman sneered. "Our pledge is withdrawn."

Emily took a step forward. "You have the wrong of it. There is a perfectly reasonable explanation for all of this," she said, fervently wishing she knew what that explanation was.

The Viscount was standing at the head of the table, eyes closed and head slowly shaking in defeat, and Emily wanted to die. This was her fault. It was all her fault. And she had to fix it, somehow. As usual, Emily's mind whirred and clicked, and an idea came to her. It was outrageous. It was risky.

But it was all she had.

"I am not unchaperoned," Emily said. "Lady Griselda is my chaperon."

"And why have *I* not been informed of this?" the harridan asked.

"Perhaps," Emily responded in a deceptively civil tone, "because it was *none of your business.*"

As Mrs. Kellerman sputtered, Emily realized she would have to go home now. There would be no position waiting for her. She could not stay at Stendmore Park, and she had no money to run. Lord Winter was right: impulsive behavior *was* a wild, unpredictable beast. One time it could lead one to sweet baby elephants, charming little girls, and gentlemen who stole one's heart, while the very next, it led to ruination.

Across from her, the harridan had subsided, perhaps sensing, as everyone else scattered about the room clearly did, that Emily had more to say. Emily looked from person to person and forced herself to smile. *Leap and the net shall appear*, she thought, and took another deep breath.

"I was sent here by my father on a matter of utmost importance," she said. "He will be glad to hear you have withdrawn your investment, Mrs. Kellerman. He will be pleased to have a larger share."

"Share?" the harridan demanded. "Share of what?"

Emily clasped her hands behind her back and paced the length of the dining room in silence. Everyone was hanging on her next words. The Viscount's future was hanging on her next words, and his children's. "This neighborhood," she finally said, "has long been known to the *ton*, but only as a sleepy village with a coaching inn on the road to Bath. The inn does a very brisk business, but none of the travelers linger. Your Lord Winter proposes to change that," she said, carefully keeping her eyes from meeting the Viscount's. "He has formulated a bold plan. A plan to transform the village, to bring economic prosperity and cultural refinement to your very doorsteps. You will no longer be forced to travel to Bath or to London to seek entertainment, opportunity, and the finest society. Indeed, those who live in either town will come to you —bringing their sons and daughters and their riches."

As a murmur of surprise floated through the air, Emily spared a glance at the Viscount. He was staring at her in shock, and she plunged on: "Lord Winter cleverly arranged to have the expensive elephant brought in as a token of his good faith, to prove to you that he meant to do as he said."

"Which is?" Doctor Brown asked.

"He means to build a pleasure garden—right here in Buxley-on-Isis, a garden to rival Raneleagh or Vauxhall, a garden full of music and light. There will be assembly rooms, a hall for presentations, a green that will host everything from balloon ascensions to fireworks, to races, and a water garden. The crowning centerpiece to these Winter Gardens will be a grand menagerie—with that adorable baby elephant as its first permanent exhibit."

The company looked from Emily to the Viscount, who stood at the far end of the table, his face an unreadable mask. He said nothing. No one did. Five seconds ticked by. Ten.

Just then, Baby reached to pilfer an ostrich feather from Mrs. Kellerman's turban and waved it joyfully about. Someone snickered.

Mrs. Robertson and then Griselda and Basil began applauding gently, and, slowly, all the guests except the Kellermans joined in.

Emily beamed. "It will be a glorious success!" she said over their applause. "A place for the weary traveler to rest his bones—and empty his pockets. Everyone who is anyone travels that road. And every last one of them would like a place more hospitable to stop. Why not give them one?"

"Why not indeed!" Sir Basil chimed. "Splendid idea! Splendid!"

The applause grew louder and Emily stood a little taller. She'd succeeded! But she thought she could do a little more. As the applause began to die down, she cleared her throat. "The Viscount has always believed pleasurable pursuits are important for a healthy mind and body, which is why he thinks it necessary to bring a pleasure garden here, seeing as how there are so many illustrious personages about and nothing *fanciful* for them to do."

"*Humph!*" Mrs. Kellerman flounced. "The Viscount is a great expert on the pursuit of pleasure —as we all know."

Emily gave her a sweet, sympathetic smile that said she thought Mrs. Kellerman was possibly the most stupid woman in all England. "While some still believe the Viscount was simply a rakehell when he was a young man," she said, "most in Town have heard he was in truth conducting scientific research. He is to be presenting a paper on the subject later this year."

But Mrs. Kellerman clearly didn't believe her

story. "And what is your postulate, my lord?" she asked.

"He has concluded," Emily answered for him, "that pleasure and personal beauty are directly connected. You, for instance, must certainly indulge in pleasurable pursuits, as your noted beauty does not come from a cream pot." She paused. "Does it?"

Mrs. Kellerman opened her mouth, clapped it shut, and opened it again before answering. "I should say not! But why all this havey-cavey skulking about? Why all this false name business and pretending to be the governess?"

"Madam, in business dealings of this magnitude, timing is everything. Were Lord Winter to reveal his intentions too soon," she said in a patronizing tone, "the deal—and the neighborhood's future—would have been spoilt. Is that what you would have wanted?"

"Why no, I—"

"And will you allow a little spilt syllabub to ruin this chance for the neighborhood to flourish?"

"Of course not, I—"

"Very well, then. I think all is settled. The misunderstanding is cleared up."

"Except for one small detail," Mrs. Kellerman

said with an acid curl of the lip. "What about your *baby*?"

"Baby?" Emily said in confused tones, giving a convincing performance. "Oh! My baby!" She tittered dramatically behind the back of her hand. "That," she said, pointing to Baby, "is *Baby Laleeta.* We call her 'Baby' for short."

Mrs. Robertson cackled. Uproarious laughter amongst the entire company erupted. Even Mrs. Kellerman's wispy husband chuckled, and Mrs. Kellerman herself had no choice but to chisel her hard features into the semblance of a smile and force a laugh—a brittle sound that told Emily beyond doubt that the lady's humiliation this day would keep her in check for years. The neighborhood would not allow her to live it down. The cat was belled.

The dining room erupted with a dozen excited conversations: *Is it not grand? The Winter Gardens! What an appropriate name! What an insightful idea!*

One old squire declared he'd always known Master David would come home to roost and make the neighborhood proud.

"He is quite the gentleman," said a matron with a gleam in her eye. She had several unmarried daughters.

"I say," Sir Basil piped into the general melee, "I have five thousand pounds I would like to invest."

"So do I," said Mrs. Robertson. "How many shares will that buy?"

The assembled crowd murmured excitedly, and Lady Griselda rose to lead the rest of the ladies into the parlor. Emily's eyes found Lord Winter's.

He was seething.

She was stunned.

Their gazes locked, and he strode around the table. "A word with you," he said tightly, gripping her arm and drawing her out of the dining room, down the hall, and into the library. He closed the door.

"A closed door, my lord? Propriety demands—"

"Propriety be damned. It wasn't enough for you to sally into Stendmore Park and turn *my* life upside down, was it? No! You had to turn the *entire village* upside down. You have committed me to building a vast pleasure garden. If I go through with it, life in Buxley will never be the same. And if I do not, I shall be reviled, and Rose and Rain will suffer for your thoughtless impulses." He shook his head. "I must not only resurrect this ruin of an estate, but I must also somehow construct a pleasure garden. All on the charity of the neighborhood."

"Loans are not charity."

"Ten thousand pounds is not enough to do the job, either. The sum is barely adequate to rescue Stendmore Park. It's not even a tenth of what I would need to construct your blasted pleasure garden! Once more, your thoughtless devotion to impulse has left ruin in your wake."

"You do not understand, my lord," she said quietly.

"I understand perfectly. With nowhere to go and no real plan of action, you skipped blithely away from your family in the middle of winter with nothing in your pocket. You stole an elephant and walked off into the country. You came to my kitchen door looking for a meal and accepted employment. And then you decided to become a governess for God only knows how much longer. You lied. You deceived. Did you think about how your family would feel to find you gone? Did you consider your employer's mortification when he discovered he'd hired some rich man's precious daughter? Did you consider your charges and how they might fare under the tutelage of an inexperienced and spoiled debutante? Did you even consider what would happen to the poor elephant if severe weather had caught you on the road with no place to stay? And what about that Banbury tale you told about my presenting a scientific paper?"

Emily had withstood the onslaught admirably, for she deserved every bit of his scorn. "My uncle Daniel is a member of the Royal Society," she said quietly. "I am sure he can be persuaded to help us. He is a good man."

"And what if he will not? Did you consider *that* before you opened your mouth? No. You considered none of it. You never do. And you have no remorse for any of it. *Do you?*"

"Everything worked out well," she said.

"For you, perhaps, Miss *Whatever*. But I see no net under my daughters," he said in bitter tones, and, turning away, he leaned heavily against the mantel.

"You do not understand," she said again. "You will have the money you need. My father is one of the richest men in England, and he will pledge any amount to see me wed and be rid of me."

He spun around to face her. "What makes you fancy I wish to wed *you*?" he said, misunderstanding her intent. "As you said, it was only a silly kiss. A momentary passion, ephemeral and soon forgotten. We are complete opposites. You are a slave to impulse, and I the architect of my own destiny. I do not even like you. Just because you announce in my dining room that your father will give me money does not mean I am obligated to wed you. I will find someone else to wed. And you—"

"Will marry the Duke of Besshire."

He stilled. The moment stretched as the mantel clock ticked off the seconds. "The Duke of Besshire?" he said. "You are to marry the Duke of Besshire?"

Emily looked down at her hands and nodded. "I —I suppose it is time I told you the truth."

He scoffed. "Do you know how?"

Emily winced. "I deserve that." She wandered over to a gold damask sofa, trying to compose herself. She wanted him to understand her. She wanted him to know why she'd been traipsing about the countryside, but she couldn't tell him everything. Oh, no ... not everything!

She took a deep breath. "In Town I am not called Emily, my lord. I am known as *Anomaly*—a name I have earned, for I learned early that when one's family sees one as an embarrassment, one is left blissfully alone in the country."

"So you acted the part of hoyden to avoid London?"

Emily nodded. "And its marriage mart." She

forced herself to smile. "I aspired to be a spinster, my lord. I always have. Unfortunately, it is apparently not at all The Thing for me to remain unwed. It is an embarrassment to my parents, and they have asked me to choose a husband. They have ordered me, threatened me, bribed me, blackmailed me, and begged me until we have all grown weary of it. But years and years ago I decided that I would never marry."

"Why?"

"My parents are incompatible and unhappy."

"Not all couples are unhappy," he said. "Some are content with their lot."

"Were you content, my lord?"

His brows slammed together, and she took that for an an answer. "Convenience is not enough inducement to marry. Nor even attraction." She walked over to the window and peered outside, but the grounds were shrouded in darkness, just like her future. "I have remained stubborn — and unwed — until now, but then, a month ago, at some crush of a rout my parents attended, my father let it be known just how much he was willing to settle upon me. He forced me to come back to London. Every Town pug with an unwed son gathered nigh, and I suddenly had more beaux than I could count, all ardently professing their undying affection.

"My father is just as stubborn as I am, and he says that as long as I remain unwed, this is the way things will be for the rest of my life. He says I am to reside in London, surrounded by insincerity and artifice, plied by greed and deception. To have any peace, I must marry."

"So you ... you will marry this Besshire? Do you love him?"

"La! Heavens no!" Emily said, deliberately glib, and she prepared to tell the most difficult lie of all. "He is rich, you see, and he owns several country estates. Love is but a silly, fleeting notion." She waved her hand in the air. "You and I both know there are more important considerations than love."

For the span of ten seconds, they stared into each other's eyes. Then the Viscount spoke, his voice a near-whisper. "So. Once more, you are leaping into the air."

He still did not comprehend. She supposed she should be grateful.

Standing suddenly, ramrod straight, she pasted on a false smile. "Indeed! I shall leap into marriage, and I am certain I shall be quite happy," she said, though she was certain she would be miserable instead. "After all, he is a duke. The highest rank that is offered—unless you think I should hold out for a prince." She gave what she hoped was a supple laugh. "I shall be the Duchess of Besshire."

He brushed his fingers across the polished surface of a library table. "If you are so set on being a duchess, why were you traipsing about the countryside pretending to be impoverished?"

"Oh … I do not know. I was bored, I suppose. I wanted to see what it would be like to be a beggar. I never expected to meet anyone I knew. What could it hurt? And then you were ordering me to become your governess, and I thought, *why not*? It was all a lark, you see?"

He stared at her, unmoving.

"Oh, do not look at me that way. You have landed in the cream! My father will happily lend you all the money you need for the Winter Gardens —and on good terms, too, as I will insist upon it as a condition of marrying Besshire. And I will also insist upon the construction of a sweet little cottage here in Buxley just for the Duke and I. Ah—very clever of me, is it not? The Duke passes through Buxley-on-Isis quite often on his way to Bath—he has a grand estate there, you know—and the Winter Gardens will provide me some amusement and a comfortable place to stay while traveling back and forth with my new husband."

At the word, "husband," she felt her eyes prick with tears. She moved toward the door. "I admit that the notion came to me quite suddenly at dinner this evening and that I did rather blurt it out. But you will own that it is a most excellent plan. We shall all live very happy ever after, I daresay."

14

MIDNIGHT

*D*AVID WATCHED HER curtsy and then she was gone.

He stood there for a few seconds, trying to order his thoughts, but they were all jumbled. He couldn't make sense of any of it. She wasn't a beggar but an heiress. A notorious hoyden. A confirmed spinster. Yet nigh on betrothed to this Duke of Besshire person.

He had never met Besshire, but he imagined a strapping fellow dressed in the first stare of fashion. Besshire obviously needed an infusion of cash if he had offered for Emily. Her breeding was not impeccable, but her father's fortune was. In return for what would certainly be an enormous dowry, Emily would become a duchess. An image of the two of them embracing flashed into David's mind, and he flinched as though stabbed. "Ugh!" He thrust the thought away and fled the library for the sanctuary of his bedchamber. But then, halfway down the hall toward the stairs he remembered his guests.

They were waiting for him in the drawing room.

Sir Basil and Mrs. Robertson's ten thousand wasn't enough to save the estate *and* build the pleasure garden, and David would be damned if he'd take a loan from a man willing to sell his own daughter for any price—even if that daughter *were* a thoughtless, capricious, scatterbrain like Emily Winthrop.

No. There would be no pleasure garden. He was going to have to go in there and announce that the "deal" was off.

He didn't know Mrs. Robertson personally, but he'd known Sir Basil since boyhood, and he wondered if Sir Basil could still be persuaded to loan him his five thousand to rescue Stendmore Park.

If not, what was he to do?

With a heavy sigh, he turned into the drawing room, feeling alone. But as he walked into the drawing room, he found himself far from alone. In fact, he was immediately surrounded. The assembled guests pressed in, jostling him.

"I say, Winter, if Sir Basil and Mrs. Robertson are in, then you must allow me to—"

"Count me in too, Winter!"

"I shall loan twelve hundred pounds."

"Three-fifty from the Smiths of Smith Hill!"

"Put me down for seven hundred."

"Are you only taking loans, or are you selling shares as well?"

"How many shares are available?"

"I will pledge as many shares as I can afford."

"I will pledge a hundred pound premium over the going price if you consider my pledge first!"

"See here, Lord Winter's father and mine were quite good friends, so I daresay the current Lord Winter shall consider *my* pledge first."

"I do not have money to throw around as these other gentlemen do, but you will be needing timber, and I have plenty of fine oak in my woods."

"I'll pledge a team of oxen and gravel from my quarry."

"I have the finest roses in the county. They're yours if you want them."

"Will you be putting up a new inn, my lord? I

should like to put my hat in as ostler," Mr. Dumfries said.

Mrs. Dumfries waved the corner of her shawl. "Tea and scones, my lord!"

The gentlemen jostled him, while the ladies clamored hardly less gently in a close ring behind their husbands. Everyone, it seemed, wanted to be a part of the Winter Gardens' success.

Within a matter of a few minutes, David's guests had pledged nearly a quarter of what he thought he would need to construct the Gardens, even without a loan from Emily Winthrop's father. With that amount, he could secure a loan for the rest.

No one cared—or even seemed to remember—that he'd been an infamous rakehell.

As though she'd been reading his mind, Mrs. Robertson poked him gently in the ribs with her fan. "I suggest you look to the rest of the inhabitants of Buxley. Even very small amounts add up quickly, and I will wager nearly everyone around will want to join in."

"Well, *I* do not wish to join in!" Mrs. Kellerman said, entering the room. She'd gone to change her syllabub-soaked gown, but still looked thoroughly disheveled. "Come, Mr. Kellerman," she ordered and, turning, waddled off toward the stairs. Her husband followed, looking like a beaten dog. "I have a megrim," she said over her shoulder in a tone designed to carry. "Pray tell your valet to pack our things, Mr. Kellerman, as we will be leaving as early as possible on the morrow!"

"But … Mrs. Kellerman …" her husband whined.

As their voices faded up the staircase and down the upper hall, the company in the drawing room stood still, collectively quivering. No one knew quite what to say.

No one but little Rain.

Though their governess was nowhere to be seen, the two little girls had somehow slipped into the drawing room unnoticed. Into the stunned silence, Rain small voice lisped, "I reckon she'll be even crosser when no one will let her into the gardens!"

Everyone in the room laughed, including David, for he realized in that moment that his title and estate were safe and his daughters' futures were out of danger. He tousled Rain's hair and directed a footman to fetch her and her sister some lemonade.

Doctor Brown clapped him on the shoulder. "Well, my lord, it looks as though Buxley will have a doctor going forward." He gave a guilty shrug. "With the recent decrease in population, I had been thinking of moving, you see, to a larger village."

A Mr. Yardley stepped up. "Ah, but there are bound to be more people here now. I daresay the village will grow in no time."

"Will the Winter Gardens build its own assembly hall?" his wife asked, stepping into the circle. "Perhaps a room that is less drafty than the old place?" she added hopefully.

"And less leaky," piped up another lady. "Every time it rains, we must cancel our assemblies or risk splashing our way through the figures."

"Indeed," another added excitedly. "Perhaps we shall be able to hold a regular assembly once more. I do adore dancing! Oh, would it not be splendid if the Winter Gardens held a subscription ball each month? If we made it fancy enough, travelers might attend."

"Rich travelers," Mrs. Yardley corrected with a laugh.

"Handsome travelers," another lady added. "We have four daughters!"

Everyone laughed and an excited murmur filled the air as the rest of his guest gathered 'round once more, all hopeful for the future, optimistic, and happy. David smiled and backed slowly out of the circle unheeded as they talked amongst themselves.

For the next half hour, merriment prevailed. In the absence of their governess, David kept watch over the Hellions, but they didn't make a false move. They were perfect angels the entire time. When they were not chatting amiably with his guests, they were staring up at him with rapturous expressions. David was even given several compliments about how well-behaved they were or how pretty they looked. They were models of English youth, proper and wholesome and good.

"They are just like their father," said an older man, gray at the temples and nodding sagely, "a little high-spirited at first, but a stalwart heart of gold when it counts." Mr. Carter was much looked up to in Buxley-on-Isis for his sage advice and straightforward demeanor. "You have done well, young man." He nodded thoughtfully. "Very well indeed."

"Thank you." David inclined his head, and Mr. Carter moved off. For a moment, David found himself alone and had an opportunity to take in the scene. The servants had done a beautiful job making the house look lovely. What little silver he had left was there in the drawing room, shined to perfection.

A hundred candles gave the room a delicate glow, the scent of beeswax filling the air. The footmen stood in attendance, perfectly liveried, keeping glasses filled and empties removed. David caught the eye of one footman and nodded his thanks. The young man, who'd been but an under gardener scant weeks ago, returned his smile before discreetly looking away. Clearly, he felt like he belonged.

And, for the first time, so did David. He wasn't an imposter anymore; he really was the Viscount. He felt like he belonged here, and it felt good, damned good.

He'd have enough blunt to save his estate, and enough to at least start on the pleasure garden. And, even if he couldn't complete the project, the neighborhood would watch him try, by Jove. He'd dedicate the rest of his life to it. His daughters' reputations would not suffer. Their futures were assured. And David's life would have meaning.

He should have been happy, but he wasn't.

Sir Basil and his lady noticed. They, along with Lady Griselda's friend Mrs. Robertson, cornered and flanked him when he stepped out onto the terrace for a breath of cold air.

"Out with it, my boy," Sir Basil said. "What is wrong?"

"You may speak plainly in front of Mrs. Robertson, my dear," Lady Griselda said softly.

David nodded. If his old friends trusted Mrs. Robertson, then David would too. It was no use hiding his feelings anyway. "Miss Jones—ah, *Winthrop!*—will be leaving soon. She is to marry the Duke of Besshire."

"*Besshire?*" Lady Griselda scoffed. "Pish-tosh! She'd sooner marry a hedgehog! That is nothing but a rumor."

"No." David shook his head. "She told me so herself."

The older people traded looks and raised eyebrows, and then Sir Basil spoke. "It is a well-known fact that she has refused Besshire many times."

His wife nodded. "He is dull. He smiles all the time and hardly ever blinks. The only two memorable things about him are his moist hands and extreme overbite. She can do better."

Mrs. Robertson tapped his sleeve with her green spangled fan. "If she has decided to accept him now, something is quite amiss. She knows her father would do anything to be rid of her. Including giving a huge sum to help found the Winter Gardens."

One of Sir Basil's bushy white eyebrows rose,

and he gave David a piercing stare. Then Lady Griselda patted David's hand, and the older people all went back into the drawing room.

The snowstorm finally diminished, and David left the party soon after. He sat up for a long while in his bedchamber, staring outside his window and listening as the party ended and the guests made their way to their rooms and the house grew quiet. The north wing, where the nursery was located, lay at right angles to wing his bedroom was in. Its windows were dark, which meant Emily and the children were almost certainly asleep, or he would have gone to question Miss Winthrop.

Why had she decided to marry Besshire? Was it as she said? Because Besshire was a duke and a marriage to him could give her freedom? Freedom from her parents. Freedom from a dreary life in London. Freedom from pursuit.

Or was it as Basil and Griselda and Mrs. Robertson obviously suspected—that she was wedding Besshire only to gain her father's support for the Winter Gardens?

Was it a convenience, as she said, or an immense sacrifice, as his elderly friends believed?

Either way, he'd behaved badly. In fact, he'd behaved badly several times.

He lay in bed for a time, unable to sleep. He'd accused her of traipsing off into the country willy-nilly, with no plan, but if his trio of mentors were right, he'd been mistaken.

As a woman, Emily Winthrop did not have the opportunities in life that he had. She did not have the freedom he enjoyed. Any deviations she made outside of the narrow vein of expected behavior would be seen as anomalous. Impulsive and unacceptable.

She could not travel unaccompanied. She could not dance more than twice with any man without people whispering. She could not hunt or shoot or ride or fence or box nor even fish without raising eyebrows. She was expected to shop or take long walks, embroider or read—though not anything too mentally strenuous—and someday, if she were biddable and obedient enough, she would become the mother of some man's child. A man she must not contradict or even appear to disagree with for the rest of her life.

How could she not chafe at such confinement?

Realization struck him suddenly. Emily hadn't run off into the country willy-nilly as he'd accused. Oh, no. She'd run off into the country with a plan. She'd hoped to ruin herself utterly, so that her bloody parents would leave her be. She'd been hoping to save herself from those sad, grasping noblemen who needed her dowry to shore up their crumbling piles. Men like the Duke of Besshire.

Or the Viscount Winter.

Abandoning his bed a little before midnight, he padded up the stairs toward the nursery. At first, he told himself that he was just checking on the Hellions, since they'd been up so late and had had so much excitement, but he threw that excuse overboard halfway there. What he really wanted was to gaze upon Miss Jones, to memorize the contours of her sleeping face. She'd distanced herself after supper, and though he knew it was irrational, he'd missed her presence at the party. And she'd be gone soon. Gone from Stendmore Park. Gone from his life.

All he wanted was one look. One peek and he'd go back to —

A *whoosh* of cold air flowed from the nursery as soon as he opened the door, though the fire was properly banked. *What the hell?* His eyes found the windows. They were open, and his daughters' beds were rumpled, but empty.

Expecting to find them all tucked into bed together in her adjoining room, he knocked at the door, but no one answered. Softly, he opened the door and peered inside. The room was dark and still and quiet. The bed was still made and empty.

Where were they?

He looked back at the open windows, only then noticing that the at the far window a bed sheet rope lay over the sill.

A thrill of alarm rushed through him, and David ran to the window and looked to the ground outside. There were no broken little bodies, but he could see footprints in the snow leading off into the darkness.

Oh God! He panicked. No wonder she'd not been seen down in the drawing room after dinner. She'd run away again. And his poor children had followed her! An image of them, lost and curled in the snow, huddled together for warmth and shivering—or worse, completely still—assailed him. And, cursing himself for a fool, David ran blindly downstairs and out the kitchen door.

She'd run away again, by the devil! She'd decided not to marry the Duke of Besshire after all. She was following another one of her buffleheaded impulses, and his poor children were following right along in her wake, with snow on the ground! Terror gripped his soul. Were they already dead?

Damn it. Damn her! And damn himself for believing she was anything but a selfish, unthinking—

As he passed the stables, he noticed a soft, faint glow of lamplight inside. It was probably Mr. Sneed or one of the grooms up late with a colicky horse or some such, but he ran inside anyway, just to check.

He saw her immediately.

She was standing calmly alone, bathed in lamplight and leaning against the rough doorway of the elephant's stall, still as the night. A soft smile graced her features.

David slowed and willed his heart to slow too. He was yet in shadow and his footfalls padded with straw, so she neither saw nor heard him approach. David came close enough to see into the stall. There, almost at her feet, lay three children and an elephant, jumbled together in a ball of arms and legs and trunk, all sleeping in the straw and covered with Emily's enormous shawl.

And there she stood, keeping watching over them all, and shivering in the cold.

All at once, he realized he'd been terribly unfair.

She hadn't been running away at all. No, it was obvious the children had sneaked out of the nursery to come visit the elephant and her little mahout and had fallen asleep.

"You are frozen," he said. Her soft smile evaporated, and turning to him quickly, she put her index finger to her lips to silence him. Taking off his bed robe, he placed it over her shoulders. "Why have you not awakened them?" he asked, more softly this time.

"I am waiting until after midnight to wake them. They will be disappointed if they are awake at midnight and Baby Laleeta does not speak."

Understanding washed over David and his heart swelled with tenderness. "Miss J—uh ... Winthrop. I owe you an apology."

"My lord?"

He took a breath. "I was wrong. So wrong. You *are* impulsive, but when it counts, you can be depended upon. You jumped into the air trusting a net to appear, but I see now that the net was already there, woven of your own intelligence, your own creativity, your own loyalty—and of your willingness to take a chance in the first place. But by admitting who you are, you have severed your net. By choosing to marrying Besshire, you are sacrificing your freedom … all for my children's happiness."

She looked down at her hands and said nothing.

"Tell me … is it foolish to hope that you make this sacrifice for me as well? Do you care for me? I cannot expect it. I haven't proven I am worthy of you."

She moved to speak, but David silenced her.

"In my quest to become responsible, I have also been unbending and insensitive. I have been so busy trying to control life that I have forgotten how to live it, how to enjoy it. But no more. You have changed me, Miss Winthrop. Please believe that."

The seconds stretched into an eternity as David waited for her to frame some sort of reply. He watched as distrust sparked to life in her lovely brown eyes, and he realized she was wondering if he were trying to replace Besshire, now that he knew she was an heiress.

"My dear Miss Winthrop … Emily, you do not have to marry Besshire. Or anyone else. I will help you find a governess position elsewhere, and, in time, you shall have a share of the profits from the Winter Gardens and therefore the means to be independent. I promise. I will be happy to draw up legal papers to attest to it. You never have to marry anyone. You can disappear into the country and live your life as you have always wanted to."

He watched as her eyes welled with unshed tears. "Thank you," she whispered. "Thank you, dear David."

Hope flared in David's heart, and for once, he followed an impulse, a wild impulse. An impulse that seemed right.

Taking her hand, he knelt before her.

Her eyes registered surprise and then confusion. "What are you doing?"

"A story. I wish to tell you a story," he said.

Finally, after a long, searching moment, she gave a nod, tentative and wary.

He swallowed. "Once upon a Christmas," he began, "there lived a lonely gentleman and his two beautiful daughters ..."

It was *their* story he told, the story of two unhappy people named David and Emily. "There were two little girls, you see, and an elephant and a little boy. There were lies and confusion. But there was also joy and … and awakening." He kissed her hand and then looked into her lovely eyes. "And, at the end," he said, his voice breaking, "David asks Emily—his dearest love, his *only* love, the woman he hadn't known he needed or wanted—to marry him."

"And what does she answer?" she whispered.

David shook his head. "I do not know. You will have to finish the story yourself."

A soft, warm smile blossomed upon her lovely face and then a hint of mischief glinted in her eyes. "I will finish it," she said, "on one condition."

"Anything."

"Promise me that you shall tell stories. Every day."

"I promise," he said. "Every day of our lives. And I swear I shall enjoy it—f you can believe the word of the notorious David *Spend*more."

"I think you mean 'the beloved David *Forever*more.'"

Standing and enfolding her in his embrace, he bent his forehead to hers. "Do you mean it? Can it be? Do you truly love me?" he asked.

She smiled and nodded. "Of course."

"Then I beg you," he said, "tell me how the story ends."

Emily laughed softly. "She says, 'Yes,' of course."

As Emily and David kissed, three children slept at

their feet. In the distance, the church bells rang through the clear, cold night air, heralding the arrival of Christmas Day.

And as the last, clear tone of the Christmas bells faded away, a lilting, girlish, and slightly nasal soprano, redolent of sandalwood and spices, whispered, "And they lived happily ever after!"

The End

or is it?

Wouldn't you love to be there when
Rose and Rain —*and Mrs. Kellerman!*—learn
that Emily is to become the Viscountess Winter?
You can be!

Come enjoy
The Further Adventures
at

www.MelyndaAndrews.com

The Further Adventures
are little stories featuring your favorite characters
from this book and others. They're Melynda's gift
to you.
To get them, you just need to tell her where to send
them.

ABOUT THE AUTHOR

Melynda Beth Andrews

Melynda Beth Andrews grew up in rural Florida, "running happily dirty and barefoot through the wild." She describes herself as highly experiential, having tried everything from flying a plane, to whitewater rafting, to diving.

She has taught English, science, art, and drama; worked as a graphic and web designer; and created over 350 large-scale abstract expressionist paintings, which she sold all over the world.

Her first novel, *The Blue Devil*, was nominated for a Golden Heart award from the Romance Writers of America and reached #1 on the Top 100 Regency Romance Bestsellers list on Amazon. Her *Regency Matchmaker Series* spent a consecutive 24 months on Amazon's Bestsellers lists. Her work has been nominated for a National Reviewers' Choice Award.

Her novels have been called "fun," "intelligent," and "wildly entertaining."

She lives her own happily-ever-after with her husband and children in the foothills of the Cascade Mountains in the United States. She enjoys hiking, reading, painting, sculpting, and learning new musical instruments—most recently, the ukelele.

Go to the author's website at
www.MelyndaAndrews.com
to learn how to get free copies of

The Blue Devil

and

Miss Grantham's
One True Sin

Books I & II of The Regency Matchmaker Series

And while you're there, don't forget

to sign up for
The Further Adventures.
www.MelyndaAndrews.com
Contact@MelyndaAndrews.com

Printed in Great Britain
by Amazon

28311779R00138